PRAISE FOR
The Mother

"A gripping tale of love and loss . . . heartbreaking and provocative. . . .
Edwards gently taps into the emotional well that we witness too often
in newspapers, on cable news, and in our social media circles. . . . [A]
tour de force that deserves recognition and as wide an audience as
possible." —Patrik Bass, *Essence*

"Edwards delivers a quietly devastating novel about a mother's attempt
to survive after the murder of her sixteen-year-old son. . . . The
book's delicate, lyrical prose belies the horrifying events that propel
the plot . . . the story of one family's road to acceptance and healing
in the wake of a tragic loss." —*Booklist*

"In this memorable story of strength in the aftermath of violent tragedy, Edwards paints a close, vivid portrait of a mother's unrelenting
mission to avoid anger and blame, instead finding real justice and
necessary closure." —*Publishers Weekly*

"A tour-de-force novel by an accomplished writer. Edwards treads
some of the same sociological pathways as she did in her first novel:
poverty, parenthood, familial responsibility. Yvvette Edwards has
written a clear-eyed, unsentimental novel about modern city life and
the challenges parents face (sometimes finding themselves the victims of tragedy). *The Mother* is another hit-the-ball-out-of-the-park
novel by a writer to watch." —*New York Journal of Books*

"A mother learns more about her murdered teenage son, and her family, than she knew possible during his killer's trial."
—*Brooklyn Magazine*

"Here are beautifully drawn characters anchored in the universal
experiences of love, loss, and grieving. With subtle nuance and elegant precision, Edwards crafts a richly detailed world that holds up
the great weight that bears down on it: the death of a child."
—*Kirkus Reviews*

THE
Mother

ALSO BY YVVETTE EDWARDS

A Cupboard Full of Coats

THE
Mother

A Novel

YVVETTE EDWARDS

Amistad

An Imprint of HarperCollins*Publishers*

HarperCollins
PUBLISHERS
Since 1817

First published in the United Kingdom, in a different form, by Mantle, an imprint of Pan Macmillan, in 2016.

A hardcover edition of this book was published in 2016 by Amistad, an imprint of HarperCollins Publishers.

HarperCollins books may be purchased for educational, business, or sales promotional use. For information, please e-mail the Special Markets Department at SPsales@harpercollins.com.

FIRST AMISTAD PAPERBACK EDITION PUBLISHED 2017.

Designed by Shannon Nicole Plunkett

Library of Congress Cataloging-in-Publication Data has been applied for.

ISBN 978-0-06-244081-5

17 18 19 20 21 OV/LSC 10 9 8 7 6 5 4 3 2 1

To:
Danielle
Nathaniel
Ella
Hannah
&
Ashton

THE
Mother

1

MY CUP OF TEA IS on the bedside table. It is where he has always left it; every morning of the eighteen years we have been married he has made me a cup of tea, brought it up, and left it on the side, and normally that's all it is; a cup of tea on the side. But today is not a normal day. Today is the first day of the trial of the man—well, boy really—accused of the murder of our son and, as a result, instead of a regular cup of tea on the bedside table, it is a steaming act of phenomenal cowardice and I will not touch or drink it.

Lloydie has left the house already. I know because Sheba is lying on our bed, and if he were downstairs, she would be too, padding around her bowls, his legs, hopeful, impatient, even if she'd already been fed. He's gone to his allotment probably, or maybe the shops. The point is he has gone somewhere else and anywhere else will do so long as he doesn't have to face me, doesn't have to discuss with me again why he will not come, because he has no words to explain to my satisfaction how the loss, the loss of Ryan, has left him so impotent that he cannot support me, even by simply being at my side.

I get dressed and comb my hair, what there is left of it, what remains of the hair I had eight months ago, flatten it down as neatly as I can, a task so small it takes hardly a minute, slip the wig over it, and make my adjustments to conceal from those who do not know me that although I am not South American, I am wearing one hundred percent natural Brazilian hair on my head. I wish I had the courage to stand before the court without it, to stand before my son's killer so he could see for himself the effects of his deed, which took but a moment, no more than a few minutes, to strip me clean of not just my only child, but everything else I had and presumed was mine for keeps.

I pass Ryan's room on the landing beside ours. Often in the mornings I go in there, like I went in there when he was alive, when my son was alive, to hurry his getting ready or shoo him down to breakfast, or check he'd packed his house keys and Oyster card. I can't quite break this habit. Even though he isn't here and there is nothing for me to check, in the mornings, I still go in there. I don't today because I never really know how it will go, how I will go, where time spent in my son's room may take me. Normally it doesn't make much difference. I can just go back to bed if I'm depressed, or if I'm crying I can carry on in there, in my room, the bathroom, any room in the house really, though I try not to cry around Lloydie, because it has become my role to support him, to be careful of my own acts of emotion so they do not precipitate his, heaven forbid they should precipitate his. Even on bad days it's okay because I am confined to my home and those feelings are confined to my home and no one expects me to do anything much or function, so it's not an issue, and normally that's okay, but not today, when I must go to court and take in evidence, listen to the presentation of facts in the language of science and law, have the worst thing that could ever have happened to Ryan, to us, taken apart and reassembled in front of a courtroom full of strangers. For that it is better I am as I am now, numb. Numb's good. I do not go into Ryan's room, because the risk of my numbness shifting is too high.

Nipa knocks on the front door like a policewoman, which is what she was before she branched off into family liaison. British-born, of Indian origin, she visited us two days after the event, has been visiting ever since. During that time she has become more a friend than an officer merely carrying out her duties, one who, never having known me at my best, has seen me at my worst. She is small in stature but tough-looking, confident, smartly dressed in civvies, with warm dark eyes that look beyond me, searching for my husband, not really surprised at his absence and with enough integrity not to make a phony pretense otherwise.

"He's not coming?"

I shake my head.

"You ready?"

"I just need to lock up."

"Take your time, Marcia, I'll be in the car."

Nipa is taking me to court and I am grateful; one less thing to worry about. She waits patiently as I get into the front passenger seat of the car and does the seat belt up around me without asking first, and it's one of the things I like about her, that she does not press me with unnecessary questions or to make decisions. I used to be good at making decisions, took it for granted completely, imagined it was one of those things that because I'd always been good at it, I would continue to be good at it, and then something like what happened to Ryan comes along and you realize some things are just temporary gifts granted for part of your life only, like the headful of hair you imagined would be yours forever that you went to sleep with one night as usual and woke the following morning to find gone, clean gone.

I say, "Thank you," though I don't have to because Nipa does not require me to remember my manners or follow decorum, which is good because I don't know where my head is anymore. So much of the time my mind is distracted or sidetracked. I thought it was a thing that happened to old people, losing their thread, going off on tangents, and here I am, middle-aged—am I even middle-aged yet? Is thirty-nine middle-aged?—and just forgetting what I was doing or the track of my thinking, and some people are good with people like that and Nipa's one of them, which is very helpful, very helpful indeed.

She has squeezed her car into a space so tight she has to go backward and forward a number of times before she can get it out. The windshield wipers are on, the sky is angry gray, the clouds weeping. Nipa moves the gear stick back and forth and her car goes back and forth, and I see a person standing in the rain on the other side of the road, a girl, inadequately dressed for the weather, in a shell suit that would be light blue if the rain had not made the hood, shoulders, and bottom of the legs dark blue, and she turns around—away—when I spot her, and though I only catch her profile for a second I could have sworn it was her, the girl without a proper name, standing in the street outside my home, just looking. Then

Nipa maneuvers the car out of the tiny space and we are on our way and the girl is out of sight.

"How are you?" she asks.

There was a time when I had a ready template for responding to that question, a "Fine thanks. And you?" "Yes, fine, thank you." "Lovely." Throwaway words used and reused with almost every person I met, and that was how it was for decades, never gave it a moment's thought, never imagined that to answer something so simple could involve such a churning inside of feelings to find words for. I've stopped trying to answer that question, flippantly easy before, impossible now, and instead give the answer I have settled for, the least complicated, a shrug.

"It's going to be okay, Marcia," she says. "We'll get through this. And I'll be with you every step of the way."

I nod then look out the window because I know she will be, that I can depend on her support, but she's wrong about the possibility of this ever being okay. All mums say their baby was the best and the smartest, I know they do, I've heard them, but Ryan really was. He smiled so much, and laughed all the time, even when he was teething, even when he was hot and the dribble was a constant flow and his poor gums so hard and red and swollen he smiled, as if he knew how much his pain distressed me and was trying to make it okay for me, even then. I close my eyes, see him again at that adorable age; sausage arms and legs and fat cheeks so delicious. It washes over me again, a familiar rolling wave of grief, never smaller, or less, or more manageable, regular and constant as the tide. What has happened can never be undone and it is the fact that it can never be undone that means it will never be okay. No, this will never be okay.

"Marcia, there'll be reporters and cameramen outside the court taking photos." I look at her, the engine is off. "Hopefully, that's all they'll do. Leave any talking to me. Just stay close, okay?"

I say, "Okay," touch the hundred percent Brazilian hair on my head, make sure it is properly in place, gather myself.

"Ready?" she asks.

I nod. She gets out of the car and comes around to my side, and I step out and underneath the protection of her umbrella as she locks the car then takes my arm, walking faster as we near the main court entrance and she puts the umbrella down; the Central Criminal Court, the Old Bailey. How many times have I seen this building in the papers, on the news, in films and series and dramas, so famous? Never once did I dream I would be visiting one day in person, wearing a wig on my head, to listen to evidence about my baby, my boy, never once.

She's right about the reporters and cameramen. They are gathered around a couple I do not recognize, who look as though they've just finished making a statement and have begun heading toward the building's entrance.

We went with Ryan to Montserrat two years ago to visit my mother, and as we were in that neck of the woods, we visited Lloydie's older sister in Jamaica as well. She kept chickens, for eggs and jerk, lots of them, about twenty maybe, and Ryan fed them in the mornings while we were there, went down to the coop with a basket of seeds and grain and any leftover bits and pieces from dinner the day before including bones, because chickens will eat anything so there was nothing my sister-in-law did not feed them. As he approached the coop, the chickens would start working themselves up, and by the time he entered they were clucking, pecking, flapping, feathered desperadoes in such a feeding frenzy you could never imagine that they had eaten quite recently and well. That's what is in my mind as we enter the media scrum.

It is actually terrifying, a scene of chaos and aggression, pushing, shouting, jostling, thrusting microphones into my face, cameras flashing, a roar of voices and lenses, and thank God there are a couple of police officers helping us, herding them aside, clearing a path for Nipa to steer me through, which she does, pulling me along behind her with one arm and pushing them out of the way with the other, till we are through the entrance and, as if we had stepped through the wardrobe and found ourselves in Narnia, we are in the court reception area, where it is calm and order prevails and my sister is waiting. As she embraces me tightly I look over her shoulder to check if that really did just happen, see the police directing the disappointed journalists back, back, back, still can't quite believe that it did.

"Bastards," Lorna says, checking my face, neatening my hair. "Are you okay?"

I nod.

"Bloody bastards!" she says.

"I'm sorry," Nipa says, "I'll see that doesn't happen again. We were unlucky with our timing. It must be a quiet news day."

"I think a sixteen-year-old boy being killed for no reason whatsoever is pretty big news," Lorna says.

"Of course it is," Nipa says. "I'm sorry. I used the wrong words."

Nipa steps over to the reception window, speaks through

the glass to the woman on the other side, and Lorna whispers in my ear, which I knew was the point she was making, "Even if he is black."

We navigate through the security checks and scans and searches, enter the large waiting area. It is half past nine and although the area is fairly packed with people, they are talking confidentially in whispers, moving around slowly, and it is as quiet as a full church hall during service. We head toward Court 16. It strikes me again, the irony of us being in Court 16 for the trial of a boy who was himself sixteen when he allegedly killed my sixteen-year-old son; stabbed and killed him dead.

We greet our solicitor, whom I know well now, Isabelle Rhodes, and our barrister, Jane Quigg, whom I have met only once before, in normal apparel, at her offices in Islington. She looks like a different person today, gowned and wigged like me—though I hope my wig is considerably less obvious. We shake hands and exchange greetings. Quigg introduces us to the black man in his early thirties who stands to her side and slightly behind her, who is also gowned and white-wigged, supporting a mass of folders with one arm, holding the other out to shake mine. His name is Henry Taylor-Myles and he is to be Quigg's junior throughout this trial.

"I'm truly sorry for your loss," he says, and he looks as though he sincerely means it. What a nice young man. His mother must be so proud.

"Thank you," I say.

We settle on the benches with Quigg, who explains to us that nothing much will happen this morning. There are legal discussions that need to take place about admissions, submissions, and agreed facts. She estimates these will probably go on for an hour or so after the jury selection has been completed. I am glad Lorna is here, my only sister, one year younger. She has been at my side throughout everything, attended every meeting, every hearing, the legal appointments. It was she who arranged Ryan's funeral really. I couldn't, and between me and Lloydie, I am the one coping best, so it goes without saying he played no part in it either. She has waded through the masses of paperwork and managed to get her head around it all when I simply could not. When we were younger, much younger, small girls, when our mother was on nights, I used to sing to her because she was even more afraid of the dark when it was just us two, and couldn't otherwise get to sleep. Then for a time, as adults, we became equals. Since Ryan, this stuff, our roles have become reversed. She watches over me and makes sure I am all right and that she keeps on top of everything. She is holding my hand. I realize I am squeezing hers, relax my grip. I have to ask the thing I want to know, and when I unintentionally interrupt Quigg, everyone allows it.

"Will he be there, from the start?"

No one asks who I mean.

Henry answers. So softly spoken. A gentle man. Lucky, lucky mum. "Yes, he will. He'll be behind a wall of glass where he can see and hear everything that's going on, and you'll be able to see him. Would you like to have a look at the court-room while we're waiting? I'm sure it'll be okay."

I have seen the courtroom already. Nipa brought me here last Friday for a visit after the court day had ended and I saw it then. I shake my head. He will be there from the start. "Do we know if he's actually going to give evidence?"

Quigg says, "Not yet. As soon as we know either way, we'll let you know."

I take a deep breath. "What about the mother?"

Nipa answers this time. "She'll be upstairs in the public gallery as well. I'll make sure she doesn't speak to you or sit beside you."

I nod. The legal team talk about the case in whispers, about strategies and documents. Nipa is leaning against the wall beside the bench, doing the thing she does so well, of being present unobtrusively. I need to focus on something else, stop thinking about myself.

I ask Lorna, "Did Leah get away okay?" My niece. Eighteen. Alive and doing the normal things you expect your eighteen-year-old to be doing; off on the great adventure of university and independence for the first time. She wouldn't be talked into attending a London uni close to home where we could keep an eye on her, make sure she was safe, chose instead to go to Nottingham, which has the highest murder rate in the country.

"Auntie, people can be killed anywhere," she had said, then hugged me.

"If leaving half the stuff you need to get you through the year at home, then phoning your mother to drop it off at the weekend as an emergency, counts as getting away okay, then yes, she did," Lorna says. "So of course, I've got to go up to Nottingham tomorrow. Why don't you come? Keep me company on the drive?"

It's strange having a weekend break so soon, hardly seems worthwhile this case starting on a Friday, just enough time to get going followed by an entire weekend to dwell on it before continuing.

"I'll think about it," I say. I don't have anything else planned but I know better than to commit myself to future events, never really know till the morning what kind of day it'll be. "I'll ring you early if I am."

"Are you nervous?" Lorna asks.

I shake my head. "I don't think so." And it's true, I'm not nervous, I'm impatient. I've been impatient for this case to begin and now it's about to, I'm impatient for it to be over, impatient for closure—if such a thing is possible—impatient to understand why my son is dead.

Nipa comes over. "We should go up to the public gallery now, in case there's a queue, make sure we get our seats. You ready?"

Lorna and I stand. I'm as ready as I can be. "Yes."

We say goodbye to Quigg and Henry and Isabelle. Henry tells me not to worry, we have a strong case and Quigg is excellent at what she does. I thank him. A court official leads us through the building to the hallway outside the public gallery of Court 16. We wait there in silence till the court session begins and the security guard allows us inside.

The public gallery is a small space crammed with three rows of seats. The security guard tells us that the first bench is reserved for family members only, which isn't very reassuring because of course family includes not only family members of the victim, in this case my son, but also family members of the boy who murdered him; the small front row is for both sets of family to share. There is a space in the courtroom I could have sat in, but I couldn't get permission for Lloydie and Lorna and Nipa as well. Even though he isn't here now, I harbor the hope my husband will come to his senses and join us. I sit in the public gallery like anyone else, the three of us at the far end, Lorna beside the wall, me in the middle, and Nipa on the other side of me like a bodyguard.

Other members of the public file into the seats behind us. Two of Ryan's friends have come along. They are young, as he was, tall boys masquerading as men, unsure how to behave in this formal space. I have fed and watered them for years, lovely boys, bright, polite. Luke leans over from the row behind, hugs me, cannot find words, just shakes his head and hugs me hard again, then composes himself, gets himself under control, sits down. The boy with him is Ricardo, who waits his turn patiently, then hugs me as well. The rows fill up behind us. I don't recognize anyone else, a number of individuals who appear to be on their own, an elderly couple dressed up as if attending an evening at the theater, and a group of four young girls who could be students of some kind or might equally well have known my son. I turn around and focus on the courtroom below us.

He is bigger than the last time I saw him, bulkier. Prison food must agree with him or maybe stodge agrees with him, and I don't know why I'm calling prison food stodge when for all I know he's probably eating a better-balanced diet than Lloydie and Ryan and I ever did. And anyway, that bulk isn't fat. The extra weight looks like muscle, solid, as if he has been working out nonstop every day and eating steroids. His face is fuller and the fullness of his cheeks makes him look younger, but there is nothing childish about the way he holds himself or the expression on his face. Tyson Manley.

Ryan went through a growth spurt that started when he was fourteen. It began one day out of the blue and just didn't stop. Over two years he went from five foot two inches to five eleven. We had to replace his wardrobe about three times. I don't know if his growth spurt had ended, will never know the exact height my son would have achieved as a man, the heights. His was the growth particular to adolescent boys, as if he'd simply been stretched on a rack, a lengthening that left him thin and gangly, slightly awkward, as if his limbs were too much, too long, as if he wasn't quite used yet to occupying more space.

Tyson Manley is not like that. He fully inhabits his frame. His body language suggests he is completely in control of every limb, every muscle, almost in command of the space around him. It is the body language of an older man, one who is established and doing well, confident and yet relaxed, and this is reinforced by the suit he wears, brown, expensive, designer, perfectly coordinated with the colors of his shirt and flamboyant tie. It unsettles me, this juxtaposition of manhood and his boyish face. He has an old scar running from the left corner of his mouth that stops mere millimeters from his eye, and it emphasizes the overall impression of a boy who means business.

He is sitting in a chair on the other side of a glass wall, between two people who look like officers of the court, but who I know from Nipa are actually employed by the prison service. His seat is at one end of the courtroom directly opposite the judge's bench on the other, and though the judge has not yet entered, Tyson Manley stares so fixedly in that direction you would think the judge was sitting there speaking to him about something totally engrossing. And although the court is filling up, with our legal team and his legal team and several clerks and a number of other people whose function I have not yet determined, despite the chatter and movement and noise, he stares ahead as if it is all beneath him, and as usual I find it unnerving. I have to say that this single quality in him is enough to convince me he did it, is guilty, because he has something in his aura of the type of person who could kill someone at six thirty, stroll home, have dinner and a hot bath, followed by an early night of unbroken sleep. That's what makes me think he's done it, his aura, and of course the fact he knows the girl without a proper name; I just don't know why. Understanding has been my problem from the start. How is it possible for my son to have been doing all the right things, that as parents, Lloydie and I, we were doing all the right things, and yet still Ryan is dead? This is the crux of my difficulty, the reason why, unlike my husband, I have to be here. I pray he does take the stand. I want to hear from his own mouth why he did this. I know it is his prerogative to speak or remain silent, but I need him to explain so I can properly understand. Perhaps if I can understand, I can come to terms with it, because so far I have not; I have not come to terms with the fact that I will never see or speak to or hold my son again. I can't get my head around how this could have happened.

Ms. Manley hasn't arrived yet though it is now just after ten. I'd feel more relaxed if she were here already. It would be over then, she could sit down and we could all move forward. Instead I am awaiting her arrival with trepidation. I am almost as obsessed with her as I am with her son. What kind of mother would turn up late to her son's murder trial? The answer is obvious; the kind of mother whose son could commit murder in the first place. I force myself to focus on the activity in the courtroom below. The public gallery is elevated above the courtroom and the view from where I sit is a good one. I am side on to Tyson Manley, which means I can study him throughout without his noticing; no expression or response shall escape me. I am also opposite the jury box, so I will be able to monitor the impact of the evidence on the jurors once the trial gets going. And I can see the witness stand and the judge's bench clearly.

The clerk who sits at the table in front of the bench gets up and walks over to the adjacent doorway and loudly says, "Court rise! All persons having any business with the court draw near and give your attendance. God save the Queen."

And everyone begins to stand, including the officers behind the glass with Tyson Manley, till everyone is standing except him, and only as the judge actually enters the courtroom does he rise slowly, as if bored with the proceedings already, and when the judge sits down, everyone else's cue to sit down, as with standing, he is the last to take his seat. It is deliberate and annoying, being difficult simply for the heck of it, and I wonder what he would have been like as a pupil at school, what it would have felt like being a teacher trying to teach him, or a mum.

Lorna whispers, "Talk about a whitewash."

I look around. Everyone in the courtroom with a part to play in this trial is white, apart from the defendant and Henry and the two prison guards. It's the kind of detail my sister never misses and that I rarely notice till she points it out. She's a charge nurse, on leave from work till this trial is over, and when people talk about slack disengaged nurses working in the National Health Service I know they've never met her. She is always awake, always aware of what's going on around her, taking in the fine detail. Despite the fact we grew up together, I've often thought there is little middle ground in our outlook, though it always fascinated me that her Leah and my Ryan were so similar to each other, you would have thought they'd been raised in the same household. People often mistook them for siblings.

"He's going to be tried by a jury of his peers," I say.

"Looking at this room, that's lucky for him," Lorna says.

I do not answer, because luck is not what I wish for Tyson Manley.

She whispers, "Here they come. Let's take a look at these peers."

They file into the courtroom below us looking not like jurors but like people at a bus stop on a warm day, holding their bags and coats, and in some cases, hats and scarves. They seem alert, excited even, eagerly glancing around the courtroom, taking everyone and everything in. There are more than twelve, more like twenty of them.

"I guess they bring in more than they need in case some are excused," Lorna whispers.

They are called up one by one. Each has their name read out to the court. The first three are white women who take their seats in the jury box. The fourth is an Asian man. He enters a whispered discussion with the judge and subsequently leaves court with his rucksack and jacket. The next is a young black woman who doesn't look much older than twenty. I can't decide, don't know if a black or white person is better at determining innocence or guilt, have no idea whether young and idealistic is better than a middle-aged mum who maybe will identify with me, or who might, on account of her teenaged son, identify with Tyson Manley. It is impossible to call.

Two white men follow. Then two more white women, a young Asian man, and an elderly black gentleman who looks bemused to find himself in these surroundings. A young white guy is next to whisper to the judge, and whatever he says is resolvable because he takes his seat in the box shortly after. Finally a white female pensioner who has nothing to whisper sits down in the twelfth seat. The jury of Tyson Manley's peers consists of five men, seven women. Of the men, one is the elderly black man, the other is the young Asian guy. Of the seven women, one is black. This is London, one of the most diverse cities in the world, yet of the twelve peers, only three of them are people of color.

I am anticipating Lorna's breath in my ear, so when it comes, I am not surprised. "Do they look like the random selection of a dozen people from your road?"

I do not answer, but the honest answer would be, they don't.

The judge temporarily dismisses the jury and the legal arguments begin. Quigg wants to present all of Tyson Manley's previous charges and convictions to the jury. She says they are relevant to the charges against him and recent, though it seems a given to me that his offenses—the full murky list of which I have seen—would be recent because he's only just turned seventeen. Guy St. Clare, defense counsel, opposes this. He says the admission of the previous convictions would be prejudicial and that it would be highly unfair for charges of which Mr. Manley has been exonerated to be presented in evidence against him. It is hard to guess St. Clare's age, he could be anywhere in his late fifties or sixties or early seventies even. His eyelids are saggy and hooded in a way that reminds me of a hawk, and when he speaks he leans slightly forward, not a lot, just enough to reinforce that impression, and his face is so red that for some reason port comes to mind and I wonder if he drinks a lot of it, imagine he does. He seems like the sort that might be found in the drawing room passed out, cravat askew, empty decanter within arm's reach on the floor beside him.

They agree that only the convictions relevant to the charges the defendant faces will be admitted. There is no need for the jury to be privy to the rest.

St. Clare wishes to submit an application for the CCTV footage of the person in a monogrammed brown sweat top to be removed from the jury bundle. He says it is not conclusive that the image is in fact of the defendant at all and that to present it to the jury as if it were could be misleading. Quigg respects the view of her learned friend. She agrees the images are not conclusive of identity and is happy for the jury to have a directive from the judge advising them of this. I am surprised at how cordial these legal arguments are. Apart from last Friday, when I visited with Nipa, I have never been in a courtroom before in my life, not even for a civil matter like debt or nonpayment of council tax, and there is something of a theatrical feel about it, like watching a period drama; the polished wood and paneling of the walls, the Victorian green leather and upholstery, the wigs and gowns and collars, the deference. I was expecting something more aggressive, I think, like the legal bloodletting I've seen in films, verbal warring, the cut and thrust of jibes. Instead I'm in a scene straight out of *Pride and Prejudice* and it feels surreal.

The jury is called back in and the judge directs the defendant to rise, which he does with his customary slowness, then he watches as his twelve peers are sworn in. The judge tells the jury that Tyson Manley stands charged with the murder of Ryan Williams. Then Quigg introduces herself and St. Clare to the jury and begins telling them the facts of this case.

"Ryan Williams was a sixteen-year-old boy who was predicted to do well in the GCSE exams he had been due to sit in May of this year. He lived with both his parents. He had never been in trouble with the police, though you will hear that Ryan Williams was in possession of a knife on the day he was murdered. He was a popular and highly respected pupil at school and a keen sportsman. His favorite sport was football.

"On Wednesday, March 18, Ryan went directly from school, which ended at three twenty-five p.m., to football training, which was held at the Sports Ground. Football training lasted two hours, from four o'clock till six p.m. At six p.m. when training had ended, he collected his school uniform and bag, exchanged the football boots on his feet for his trainers, left the Sports Ground with a group of other young boys his age, and they walked to HFC, a chicken and chip shop on the high street nearby. While at HFC, Ryan realized he had left his football boots in the changing room at the Sports Ground. He bought himself a meal of eight hot wings and chips and separated from his friends outside the shop. The other boys continued their journeys home while Ryan walked back to the Sports Ground to retrieve his boots."

I feel Lorna's hand in my lap. She finds mine. Holds it.

"On the way back into the Sports Ground, Ryan met Kwame Johnson, the football coach who had led the training session. Mr. Johnson was on his way out of the Sports Ground, carrying balls and equipment to his car. He asked Ryan if he wanted a lift home and Ryan said no. He had no need of a lift as it was only a short distance from his home.

"As he exited the Sports Ground, Mr. Johnson passed an individual he believed to be the defendant, Tyson Manley, on the street. Although he continued to his car, where he loaded the equipment, Mr. Johnson then went back to the Sports Ground to make sure everything was okay.

"At the entrance, a woman who had been jogging in the park, Nadine Forrester, literally ran into him. She shouted words to the effect that someone had been stabbed. Mr. Johnson ran into the Sports Ground, where he discovered Ryan Williams lying on the pathway in a pool of blood. He checked for breathing and on finding no signs of life, carried out CPR till the paramedics arrived and pronounced Ryan Williams dead at the scene.

"You will see in your jury bundle, exhibit one, on page three, a map of the Sports Ground and the surrounding area. It gives you an idea of the geography but does not give much detail. If you go to page four, you will see a more detailed map of the Sports Ground. It shows the football pitches, the changing room, the entrance to the park at the top of the page slightly to the right of the center. You can see where Mr. Johnson's car was parked outside the Sports Ground on the adjacent high street, and it is marked 'number one.' You can see the spot, marked 'number two,' at which Ryan Williams was stabbed and where he subsequently collapsed and died.

"If you go to page seven, you will see images of the stab wounds Ryan Williams sustained, not actual photographs but body graphics that will help you understand the extent of the injuries. On the back body image you will see there are four incised wounds. One of these is labeled 'three' and is in the middle upper left back region. That incision wound punctured the lung, causing it to fill with blood and subsequently resulted in loss of life . . ."

I am hyperventilating. Though I am gulping in air, I cannot breathe. It feels as though no oxygen is entering my lungs despite the fact that I can hear myself sucking it in, gasping.

"It's okay, it's okay, . . ." Lorna is saying. "You need to slow down, take a deep breath in, hold it, let it out. And another, deep in, hold it . . ."

I have attracted the attention of the jury, the legal teams, the judge; they all look up at the gallery.

Nipa asks, "Do you want to go outside?"

I shake my head, inhale deeply, feel oxygen return to my body. I am angry with myself, not for not coping, but for not coping in front of Tyson Manley. I feel like he has already taken so much from me and truly did not want to give him this in addition, my vulnerability, the confirmation that however this trial ends he has already won, already made it nigh on impossible for me to ever breathe normally again. But when I look at him, wondering if he's enjoying this scene, to see if he's snickering and smirking, he is doing neither. His attention is fixed on the judge as before, as if he is oblivious to everything, including me.

"She's okay," Lorna says to Nipa.

The judge says, "Counsel, might I suggest you continue with your opening statement?"

"Thank you, My Lord. I shall endeavor to be as brief as possible. Members of the jury, when the police arrived at the scene, Mr. Johnson, the football coach, told them he had seen Tyson Manley entering the Sports Ground as he was leaving it. They went to Mr. Manley's parental home, where he resides with his mother and younger brother, were unable to locate him there, and kept his home under surveillance throughout the night.

"The following morning, on March 19, Mr. Manley arrived

home freshly bathed and wearing newly purchased clothing. He told the officers he had been at the home of his girlfriend, Sweetie Nelson, from the previous afternoon till that morning. If you look at page three of jury bundle exhibit two, you will see itemized calls made from Ryan Williams's mobile phone— telephone one—to telephone two of various dates and durations up to and including Wednesday, March 18, the date on which he was murdered. Telephone two is the mobile phone belonging to Sweetie Nelson. If you turn to page four, you will see itemized calls made from Sweetie Nelson's phone to Ryan Williams's mobile phone, of various dates and durations, the last of which occurred two days prior to the murder. When questioned by police, Sweetie Nelson provided a statement corroborating Mr. Manley's assertion that for the period during which Ryan Williams was killed, Mr. Manley was at her home with her and that he did not leave her home till eight a.m. the following day. Tyson Manley also made a prepared statement to the police, effectively a blanket denial of any knowledge of or involvement in the murder of Ryan Williams. Subsequently, Mr. Manley was arrested and arraigned on the charge of murder.

"Before you can convict, there are three things you have to be sure of. The first is that Tyson Manley, the defendant in this case, did a deliberate and unlawful act. You have to be sure that at the time of committing the act, the defendant intended really serious injury. You also have to be sure that the act resulted in the death of Ryan Williams. These you will decide once you have heard all the evidence in this case. Thank you."

As Quigg sits down, St. Clare stands. It is almost twelve thirty and St. Clare advises the judge that he has a minor legal matter to address that should take no more than fifteen minutes. The judge suggests the jury be discharged for an early lunch and that they resume sitting at 13:55. It feels as though the case has already been ongoing an age as we leave, and having wondered about the point of the case beginning on a Friday, I find myself gratefully anticipating the weekend and the time to work on finding the strength I am going to need to see this through.

We leave the court amongst a large group of other people and are unmolested by the media, who have set up shop on the other side of the road and appear not to notice us as we slip away to a nearby pub for lunch. We study the menus awhile then Nipa goes off to the bar to order. I feel like I have been through a mangle, so distraught already and the case has barely begun.

"I don't know how I'm going to get through this," I say to Lorna. "It's so hard. . . ."

"I know," she says. "But we will get through this, for Ryan, we must."

"I can't believe Quigg mentioned that knife. Why did she mention it? It made him look bad and he wasn't. Ryan never carried a knife, ever."

"I think it's good she mentioned it, got it out of the way. Otherwise the defense would have brought it up and it would've been worse, like we had something to hide, and we haven't . . ."

Ryan was a talker, the opposite of Lloydie; my God, my boy could talk for England, even more when he was alone with me. I never really talked to my mother when I was growing up. We were not close. I was born into a "children should be seen and not heard" generation and my mother took that aspect of parenting seriously. The priorities for her generation were to ensure they didn't raise children too facety, who had manners, remembered to say please and thank you, who knew their place and didn't butt into big-people conversations, children who did what they were told when they were told to do it; no, I was not close to my mother, I was obedient.

Then I met and, after a period of courtship, married Lloydie, left home and moved in with him, and discovered he wasn't much of a talker and that was okay, because he was a considerate husband and a good listener to the things I had to say. I never even knew there had been a factor lacking, that I had never in my life before been truly fulfilled till after Ryan was born and began learning to talk.

Ryan and I talked about everything; those little ups and downs when he was three, four, five, the angst of his friendships, minuscule upsets that might have been so easy to dismiss or brush aside we discussed as gravely as a consultant might discuss a terminal prognosis with a patient. And I wanted to, *wanted* to enter his world, so sparkling and vital and innocent, so vast and unchartered, wanted his childhood to be different to my own, warm and full. When he was older, we talked about knives; no sensible parent of a teenage boy wouldn't. We talked about other people carrying them, how ridiculously easy they made it for slighted and hormonal boys to write off not only someone else's life, but their own lives and futures, in a single hotheaded moment. Ryan knew all the pitfalls and he had never carried a knife, never.

"It had to've been planted. That murderer planted it on him. That's the only thing that makes sense to me."

"Marce, Ryan wasn't some hoodie up to no good. The defense can do what they like, they can't make him look bad. The jury will get it. Don't worry." Lorna pauses then asks, "That girl, Sweetie, what's she like?"

I know she's trying to shift me, stop me focusing on the knife, move the conversation onto ground she imagines is less fraught for me, but there are only a handful of subjects less fraught for me and Sweetie Nelson is not one of them. The more I think about it, the more certain I am that it was her I saw this morning on the road outside my home. I just don't know why she was there. To speak to me? Intimidate me?

"Did I tell you how she got her name?" I ask.

"Don't think you did."

"When she was born, even after nine months of pregnancy, the mother still hadn't come up with a name for her. Some sister on the postnatal ward picked her up one day and said, 'Hi, sweetie.' Imagine that, 'Hi, sweetie.' She must've said it to every baby she touched that day, probably said it to every baby she ever touched in her career, and that girl's mother thought, 'That'll do. I'll just nip out quickly and slap it on the birth certificate so she'll be stuck with a term of endearment instead of a name for the rest of her life.' "

"That's really sad."

"She's like what you'd expect from someone from those beginnings: low."

"Bit harsh, Marce. You can't call the girl low for choices she never made."

"She's Tyson Manley's alibi."

"I know. I'm just saying you can't judge people by the decisions their parents made."

"Parent. Singular."

"Great! Now you're the bloody morality police? I'm a single parent as well, remember?"

"I'm not talking about you, I'm talking about Sweetie's mother."

"I'm just saying that . . ."

"Look, I don't need to be educated. Stop talking to me like I'm one of your bloody patients!" I get up from my seat, aware of the exact degree of my overreaction. The million and one things in my life I am angry about do not include Lorna. There are so many other people I wish I was shouting at, but I'm not, because none of them are right here at this moment supporting me. I should apologize, but I don't. Instead I pick up my bag. "I'm going to the toilet," I say.

Lorna stands to go with me.

"On my own!"

I lean against the wall inside the cubicle trying to compose myself, to calm down. During my pregnancy, I read the *Dictionary of Baby Names*, from Aaron through to Zuriel. I didn't know whether I was having a girl or a boy so I studied names for both sexes. I wanted a solid name to see my baby through life while keeping every option open. With a name like Ryan, my son could have been a footballer, which was one of his dreams, or a solicitor, which was another; he could have worked in a fried chicken shop fulfilling one of his fantasies, or become the distinguished Dr. Ryan Williams, fulfilling one of my own. I wanted a name that presented no boundaries to his life choices, with meaning as well as a lovely sound.

The name Ryan means "little king"; if he'd been a girl I would have named her Estelle, "a star."

Nipa is back, sitting beside Lorna when I return. She smiles at me and moves over, creating a space for me to sit between them like a sandwich filling.

"They didn't have egg mayo," she says, "so I just chose a couple of different baguettes and hoped they'd be okay."

"Thanks," I say, picking up the glass of white wine on the table beside the baguette in front of me.

"I left you the tuna-sweetcorn," my sister says, giving me a fairly hard poke in the side with her elbow. It's how she would have done it when we were children, discreetly, with no outward sign to alert any adult in our midst to her actions. The tuna-sweetcorn would have been my preference and she knows that, just as I know that it would have been her first choice for herself. My anger has completely dissipated. Mocking offense, I elbow her back. I say, "You would!"

2

KWAME JOHNSON IS FORTY-TWO AND has been coaching Ryan's football squad since Ryan started playing regularly at eight. Ryan always liked and respected him, and as a consequence, so have I. Many of the boys he coaches are Afro-Caribbean and he is hard on them, dishing out punishments for lateness or attitude or bad sportsmanship, balancing this zero-tolerance approach with a wicked sense of humor. All the boys call him "sir" and his relationship with them is great.

The first time I ever saw Kwame dressed in anything other than sports gear was at Ryan's funeral. That day, those awful days around it, meld in my mind into a Valium haze, but I remember my surprise, later on, at the wake, when I realized it wasn't the drugs making Kwame look so different, it was the first time I'd ever seen him formally dressed. I'm reminded of that day looking at him now, standing in the witness box, wearing a suit. As usual, his dreadlocks are pulled back into a ponytail that falls midway down his back and they are the only thing about him that feels normal. His eyes dart around the courtroom taking everything in. His expression is solemn.

Quigg is in her element. She exudes confidence, has everything under control. We learn Kwame's age and occupation, that he's been coaching for almost nineteen years, and that, in addition to the training he does in the evenings at the Sports Ground, he works with excluded kids in special schools and pupil referral units. In fact, it was at a pupil referral unit two years ago that he first met the defendant. I wasn't aware of that. I never really thought about how Kwame knew Tyson Manley, but if I had thought it through, a pupil referral unit would have been exactly where I would have imagined their paths had initially crossed. Kwame coached him as part of a group once a week, excluding school holidays, for a period of six months, up until a year ago.

"And when you stopped coaching him, was it because your coaching contract came to an end?"

"No."

"You were still coaching other young people at that same pupil referral unit?"

"Yes."

"Would you please then tell us why the coaching stopped?"

I feel Lorna nudge me as a woman is steered to a seat at the end of our row. It is Ms. Manley, who has finally showed up to support her son. I have seen her before at the hearings when her son was charged, denied bail, but we have never spoken. She is late for the afternoon court session, alone, and wearing celebrity sunglasses. She sits down and puts her designer handbag on the seat beside her, pulls off her scarf, her coat, drapes them over its top. I can smell her perfume from where I am sitting. I'm sure everyone in the gallery can.

Kwame is saying, "Tyson stopped coming. His attendance had always been a bit iffy. In the end it just kinda petered out."

Tyson Manley has noticed his mother, gives her the briefest of smiles, returns to his normal expressionless poise, continues watching Kwame in the box. You might almost think he was oblivious to everything going on around him. His acknowledgment of his mother is the first indication I have had that he is not.

Quigg asks, "Would you say that during the time you coached Mr. Manley you came to know him well?"

"I suppose so."

"Mr. Johnson, do you recall making a statement to the police on March 19, on the morning following Ryan Williams's murder?"

Kwame nods his head.

"Please answer aloud."

He clears his throat. "Yes."

"In that statement you said that you had tried very hard to build a relationship with the defendant because of his family circumstances."

"Yes."

"Would you please tell the court what these were?"

"I knew his brother, the older one, Vito. He got killed, shot in front of the family, two, three years ago. After that Tyson started getting in trouble and didn't seem to be able to get out of it. I guess I kinda wanted to help him."

"Thank you. Would it be fair to suggest you had a special interest in the defendant?"

"Yes."

Kwame is the sort who would. He had an interest in all the kids. I think about Ryan at fourteen. Under duress, we bought him his first mobile phone when he was eleven, replaced it with a smartphone for his fourteenth birthday.

Then I spent months worrying about him watching porn on it, being bullied on Facebook or social media sites, talked about the permanence of everything that goes onto the Internet, that nothing should ever be sent to friends that he would not want to see hung up on display during whole-school assembly, especially pictures of his willy with some girl's name wonkily written on it in felt tip (this last was a result of an article I'd read in the paper about young people texting photographs of intimate body parts to people they fancied). Maybe while we'd been having those discussions Tyson Manley's brother was being gunned down, Ms. Manley was identifying her son's body in the morgue, burying him, another statistic, just another young murdered black boy to add to the tally. One son dead and the other on trial facing life, another day, just another chapter in the dysfunctional life of this family. I watch her, straining my eyes in their sockets so I don't have to noticeably turn my head, wanting to see whether she is moved, teary-eyed, at this disclosure. The sunglasses make it difficult to gauge her feelings. They render her face as expressionless as her son's.

Thus far Quigg has merely been setting the backdrop. Now she steers Kwame to that day, that terrible day that began so normally but by its end changed everything in my world, the day I am still trying to understand, that my husband can't bring himself to face.

Training practice was normal. They finished at six precisely. He is confident of the exact time because he's very strict about timekeeping, thinks punctuality is an important message to send to the kids he works with. Afterward, everyone went straight to the changing rooms except him. He hung around and had a discussion first with a new parent who was hoping to sign her son up for his sessions. He gave her times and prices, went to the changing room, chatted with the boys briefly as he collected his bags, then went back out to pack up his balls and equipment, get it all ready to take to the car.

Everyone seemed normal. There were no unusual tensions. The boys shouted goodbye to him as they were leaving the grounds, including Ryan. For the next ten minutes Kwame finished gathering his gear together, hoisted it all up, then started walking to his car.

The discussions of the lighting go on for some time. It was mid-March. Sunset on that evening was at ten past six. There were no lights directly onto the football pitch, but light was cast from the lampposts along the pathway. The jury is directed to the detailed Sports Ground map, where the lampposts can be seen along the borders of the path, twenty-five meters apart. As you head toward the high street, there is also lighting from the street. Here the road is well lit, the lampposts twenty meters apart, with additional lighting from cars and traffic and the shops and flats on the other side. It was not as bright as day, but visibility was good. Kwame is still on the path, nearing the exit, when he sees Ryan walking back along the path toward him. He's eating chicken and chips. He appears relaxed, nothing untoward in his bearing. He tells Kwame he's left his boots in the changing room. Kwame says he'll wait for him, give him a lift home. Ryan says it's fine, it's only a five-minute walk, he'll see him next week.

These are the moments, the minutiae of which have consumed me these last seven months, going around and around my mind till I thought I would be driven mad, the moments when normal things were done and casual words said where microscopic alterations would have changed the direction of everything to come. If Kwame had been slower gathering his bags and balls and equipment, he would still have been at the murder site when Tyson Manley caught up to Ryan, he could have stopped him, and my son would still be alive. If Ryan had been as forgetful in the afternoon as he had been that morning, if he had not remembered the boots he'd left behind in the changing room, forgotten about them till he had PE at school two days later, or football practice the following week, by then he would probably have discovered they'd been nicked and I could have scolded him for being irresponsible while I bought him a brand-new pair and he promised to take better care of them, and he would still be alive. If Ryan had accepted the lift Kwame offered him, if Kwame had insisted despite Ryan's refusal and taken him home, if it had been raining that day and training was canceled, *any* of these, if any of these had happened, my son would still be alive.

Instead, as Ryan passed him, making for the changing room, and Kwame exited the park and turned left, headed toward his car, he saw a figure wearing a brown sweat top monogrammed in gold, and the lights from the other side of the road that illuminated the back of the hood simultaneously cast a shadow over the wearer's face, obscuring it. The person crossed the road at an angle that landed him on the pavement so he was now behind Kwame, who looked back. Despite not being able to see the person's face, he knew it was Tyson Manley.

Quigg directs the jury to bundle number two and a photograph of Tyson Manley in a brown top monogrammed in gold, lifted from his Facebook page, posted at the end of February, almost three weeks before Ryan was murdered. She asks him to confirm if this was the top the person was wearing, and Kwame says yes. In the picture Tyson Manley is with a group of four other boys whose faces have been blurred for today's purposes, posing like gangster rappers in a forceful expression of teenage masculinity. It is the kind of photograph I have seen in the newspapers when some young person has died and there is an implication that either the victim or the perpetrator was involved in gangs. I scan the faces of the jury as they look at the image, can feel at least three of them, including the elderly black guy, mentally concluding that Tyson Manley is a gang member, but I don't buy it myself, not on the evidence of one photo. My Ryan was at an age where he was always trying to look cool in photos, desperate to get rid of those he didn't think depicted him as the man he wanted to be seen as by the world. Those same jury members would probably be thinking *gang* if they saw a photo of my son with Luke and Ricardo. It's not that I reject the notion of Tyson Manley being a gang member, I wouldn't be surprised if he was, just that even I, and I have every reason to think badly of him, even I can see the association being perpetuated here, and I'm uncomfortable with it.

Quigg points out that there are probably hundreds of young men in London who own that exact top, asks, "Without seeing his face, how could you be sure that the person you saw was the defendant?"

Kwame answers, "Everything. The height, the build, the way he walked . . ."

"What was it about the way he walked that identified him?"

"He always walked really fast and had a kinda bounce. Lots of the young guys bounce when they walk, but his was very pronounced."

"Could you have been mistaken? Could it have been anyone other than Mr. Manley?"

"It was Tyson. I could have identified him anywhere, as long as he was moving."

"Did you see where he went after he passed you?"

"Into the Sports Ground. I looked back after he had passed, saw him go into the Sports Ground."

"Then you continued to your car?"

"Yes."

"Put all of your equipment into the boot?"

"Yes."

"Closed it?"

"Yes."

"Got into the driver's seat?"

"Yes."

"But you did not drive off?"

"No."

"Would you please tell the court why you did not drive off?"

"It's hard to explain . . ."

"Please try."

"I just had a funny feeling. I knew it was Tyson and he must've seen me. It was weird that he didn't say 'yow,' wasn't like we'd had a fallout or anything. In fact, it kinda seemed like he'd avoided me, deliberately kept his head down so I couldn't see his face. He was walking really fast, even for him, kinda hyped. I don't know, it was all a bit weird and I knew Ryan was still at the Sports Ground on his own. The whole thing just gave me a bad vibe."

"So you got out of the car and went back?"

"Yes."

"Did you run?"

He pauses then answers, shaking his head, "No."

"You walked?"

"Yes."

"And what happened next?"

"When I got to the entrance, a woman ran into me full force, nearly knocked me down. She was terrified, looking behind her like she was being chased."

"And did that woman say anything to you?"

"She was screaming, about an ambulance, to get help. I think she said, 'He's got a knife.' I wasn't listening properly. I was already running."

"Into the park?"

"Yes."

"Along the path?"

"Yes."

"And what did you see?"

"Ryan was on the ground. There was blood *everywhere*. I could see from the off it was bad . . . proper bad."

"What happened next?"

"I ran over to check his breathing. He was on his front and I turned him onto his back. I was scared I would damage him even more but I couldn't feel a pulse and he had to be on his back for me to do CPR. I was shouting for help between breaths while I was doing compressions . . . I just couldn't make him breathe. I knew it was too late but I had to try."

"Was there anyone else around at that time?"

"I didn't see anyone." He has been speaking to Quigg, addressing his answers to her while glancing at the jury occasionally, but now he faces the jury directly and says, "I should have run, from the moment he passed me I should have run. I don't know why I didn't, I just don't know why."

The judge asks, "Mr. Johnson, would you like a short break?"

Kwame wipes his eyes, takes out a tissue, blows his nose, shakes his head. The what-ifs are the worst of it. I know the depressing slide of that ride and I feel guilty that I have been thinking only of myself, so wrapped up in my own grief and Lloydie's that I never gave a thought to anyone else, to any of those other people first to the scene. It was as if the trauma started later, with a knock at the door and the lift in a police car to identify my son's body. I've been where Kwame is, such an easy place to get stuck. The what-ifs are infinite, a useless spiral stairway descending straight into hell. What if Kwame had done something other than what he actually did? What if he'd taken more time with Tyson, maybe gone to his house a year ago when he stopped showing up at the pupil referral unit? What if he'd told that parent to come back some other time and sat instead in the changing room with the boys like a mother, checking that everyone had packed everything? What if the what-ifs are nothing more than a coping mechanism, nothing more than a diversion from the onslaught of guilt and grief?

Lorna hands me a tissue. I wipe my eyes. I hear someone else blowing their nose. It is one of the jurors, the older woman, the final juror. She looks like a grandmother, an indulgent grandma, wiping her eyes now because she is crying too, and she is not the only juror brushing tears aside. But Tyson Manley is not crying. As I watch, he yawns. He makes no effort to lower his head or cover his mouth, just yawns as he might do while perched on the edge of his prison bunk, and the opening of his mouth is accompanied by a stretch of his arms into the air, and when he brings them back down, he rolls his head around on his neck like he's a doing a warm-up. He adjusts his tie, loosens it, undoes the top button on his shirt, then settles and is as he was before. He doesn't do it to annoy, to wind me up or offend the court, it is a natural act. He's been sitting in that chair all day and his limbs must be screaming from the stress of such a lengthy period of inactivity. I'm sure he's genuinely feeling stifled, yearning for a little fresh air. He must be, because I am. He is heedless of the jury members watching him, and it is clear from their expressions that that yawn has cost him.

Kwame continues. No breathing into my baby's precious airways or compressions to his failed heart could bring him back, though Kwame did not give up till the paramedics arrived, then watched as they tried themselves and likewise failed. He gave a statement to the officers at the crime scene where he named Tyson Manley, and the following day he went to the police station where a full statement was given and signed.

By the time Quigg has finished asking her questions, it is almost four thirty, and the judge adjourns the case until Monday morning at ten. Ms. Manley is the first to leave, snatching up her belongings, leaving the gallery swiftly without looking anyone in the eye. Though she is only a few seconds ahead of us, there is no sign of her in the corridor outside the gallery entrance. She obviously has the art of the clean getaway down pat. Perhaps I would also be an expert at leaving fast if I had raised my son to kill.

The cameras of the media flash mutely from the other side of the street as we leave with Lorna. Nipa drops the two of us back at my house, where I hug her before she departs, for everything, picking me up, coming along, being a solid and uncomplicated support to my world. I let myself in through the side door that opens directly into the kitchen. It feels warm and smells of recently cooked food. It is almost six. I take my coat and Lorna's out into the hallway to hang them up and shout up the stairs, "Lloydie? Lloydie!"

On the mat inside the front door there are a few letters, which I leave, apart from one, obviously a card delivered by hand. I open it. On the front it says "Thinking of You." It is from my neighbors, a very elderly couple who live next door, Rose and Dan. Ryan used to knock every evening to check if they needed anything. When he was younger, I used to remind him to knock, but as he got older, he took responsibility for remembering and popped around happily. With my mother in Montserrat and Lloydie's father so disconnected from our lives, they were the closest thing Ryan had to grandparents and they loved him to bits. They cried like close family when they found out he'd been killed. They are in their eighties and I'm confident his death has taken years off the finite number they had left. Amongst the things I wish, I wish Tyson Manley could be made to meet them, to explain to them how best they might accommodate their grief. Presumably he is able to compartmentalize his life, to detach the death inside it from the living parts. I wish he could see the life he's left me with, the way those two parts have been forged into one.

I read the card. A simple hope for the strength we need to get through this. I feel a lump forming at the back of my throat. It is always these little things that undo me. I swallow and take the card back into the kitchen with me, put it up on the window ledge beside a photo of my son.

Lorna is holding the raised lid of the doving pot in one hand and pops a piece of meat into her mouth with the other. She looks at me, closes her eyes. "Mmm . . ." she says, "that's good." Then, more of a statement than a question: "He's not here?"

I shake my head. Sit down. She goes to the cupboard, takes out two plates, opens the pots, and dishes up dinner for us both. I pull off my shoes, flex my toes, take off my scarf, cardigan, wig.

"Different people deal with things differently," she says.

"He's not dealing with anything."

"This is his way of coping."

"He's not coping."

"He's doing his best, Marce. Sometimes it's hard to see but most people are just doing the best they can in the circumstances they find themselves in."

I wave a hand dismissively. "Give it a rest."

"Do you want me to put yours in the microwave? It's kinda lukewarm. I'm happy to have mine like that, but I know you like your food nuked till it's too hot and you have to blow and wait for it to cool down for two hours."

"Yes, please," I answer. She's trying to fill the space with normal chatter, and I want to rise to it, to meet her partway, but it requires energy I cannot find. As she puts my plate into the microwave and her own onto the table and goes to collect cutlery for us both, I get up, take out an opened bottle of vodka, grab a couple of tumblers and a carton of cranberry juice from the fridge, and pour. Lorna puts my plate in front of me, sits down, starts eating.

"This is one of the advantages of having a husband, coming home to find the dinner's cooked."

"It shouldn't be the only advantage."

"Marce . . ."

"I know. Okay."

"Don't you think there's a kind of natural progression between seeing your brother gunned down in front of your eyes and growing up to be a killer?"

"It's very sad."

"It's heartbreaking. Y'know, some of these kids' lives are like a war zone. They see things that would give adult soldiers PTSD and it's like somehow they're just expected to absorb it and carry on; rinse the blood off your jacket, go to school, play football, skate. I bet that boy never received a day's counseling in his life."

"I have to admit, I forgot to inquire."

"And there's still another younger brother coming up."

That's true; another sibling who has had his eldest brother shot dead, the middle brother a killer himself. What a legacy. What must that child be like?

Lorna asks, "Aren't you going to eat anything?"

"I'm not really hungry."

"Got space for the vodka though."

I take a deep breath, look at the plate she has placed in front of me. She has given me a chicken thigh, which will need to be cut. I look at the table knife lying innocuously beside the fork, know I can't do it. Sitting through the case today has brought me close to images in my mind of knives slicing through flesh that need internalizing again, and distance. I put down the glass, pick up the fork, move the piece of meat to one side, feed myself a mouthful of rice with gravy, resist the urge to open my mouth after swallowing, extend my tongue, show Lorna that the contents of my mouth are truly gone. I look away as she begins sawing easily through the breast on her own plate.

"I wish I could stay," she says.

Leah has a cat, Ashanti, that she hasn't taken with her to Nottingham, that requires feeding, watering, letting in and out.

"It's fine. Wouldn't want your ear to the wall while me and Lloydie were getting our groove on. Probably be off-putting."

"I think you mean off-putting for me."

I swallow the food in my mouth, take my time responding. "Whatever."

"What are you gonna do?"

"Have a long bath. Watch telly. Stroke the cat."

"Fun stuff."

Yes, fun stuff. I'll sit here alone in silence waiting for what's left of my husband to come home, even though I know he won't be back till late, because he knows what he's doing is wrong, but he can't do differently, and because of that can't face me. I hope my smile doesn't look like I feel. "Exactly."

Lorna leaves after we have eaten, after the phone rings and she hears me say, "Hello, Mum," indicating with her hands I shouldn't mention she is present, snatching her bag and planting a goodbye kiss on my forehead, then is out the door so swiftly that even if I'd wanted to, there is no time for me to press her to reconsider. I was always the obedient daughter and she was the headstrong one. Though younger than me, she left home before I did, using university as her vehicle. She doesn't share my sense of duty, does not endure anything with anyone, from partners who almost make the cut to mothers too set in their ways to bend.

"How are you?" I ask my mother.

She answers, "Alive. What happened in court?"

My mother retired to Montserrat, five years ago. She spent her working lifetime putting every penny she could into building a house there, working double, sometimes triple shifts around the clock and around us, then watched for over a decade the effects of the volcano on the tiny emerald isle, the evacuation of most of her old friends and family to the far reaches of the world; was grateful she had built in the north of the island, one of the areas least affected, that she still had a home in a hot place to retire to.

Speaking to her is not an emotive process. She is a woman who deals in facts. I use the language of the courtroom to tell her about today's developments and she listens, interrupting only to ask for clarification of the occasional detail. She has never been led by her feelings, in fact the only time I have ever known her to be overcome by her feelings was the morning, the day after Ryan was taken, when I rang and told her he'd been murdered. Even though I was in the act of informing her, I was still in a state of denial. I had been to the hospital the evening before and seen him, my beautiful boy. All the damage was to his back, and because he was lying on his back when I looked at him, he could simply have been asleep. So when I phoned my mother, the words were coming out of my mouth mechanically while a voice inside was screaming that he couldn't be dead, a mistake of some kind had been made, though it was impossible to fathom how and just what the mistake was. When I told her what had happened and she cried, it was the first time I'd ever heard her cry, and because of it, that was the moment I realized there had been no mistake, that Ryan was dead, that it was true. By the time she got here for the funeral, those feelings had been packaged and compartmentalized. She went into action directing, organizing, sorting things out with Lorna, cooking and freezing so much food for us before she left that it took us months to eat it all. Her response to calamity is to get busy. Ironically, her lack of emotion has made her one of the easiest people to discuss Ryan with.

When I have finished with the day, she says she will phone back on Monday, and says to say hello to Lloydie. As I put the phone down, it rings again straightaway. I answer. It is Leah, my niece, wanting to know how it went and how I am. She is the opposite of my mother, talks about her feelings and wants to know about mine. She is upset to not have been with us today, explains to me, as though I don't already know, that she had to enroll, move her stuff, but is hoping to come back to London on Tuesday evening and come to court with us on Wednesday. I force a promise from her that she will not do this, that she will concentrate on her life, her course, her future. She can ring me every day and I will tell her how it's gone, but I don't want her compromising her studies one bit. Then she tells me about her day, her "cozy" bedsit, her en suite, the smallness of which she describes in such detail that she makes me laugh, blessed girl, properly, out loud.

When that discussion ends and I put the receiver back down, it immediately begins to ring a third time, and I am tempted to ignore it, in fact I do for a while, but it doesn't stop. We disconnected the answering machine in the weeks following the event. There were so many messages every day and I could hardly concentrate enough to listen to them, never mind return the calls. Many were from journalists, and people I barely knew. The answerphone became an additional stress so we disconnected it and have not reconnected it since. Because of that, people determined to get through can hold on forever and what happens is what's happening now; instead of being able to ignore it, I start to wonder if something has happened, perhaps to Lloydie, wonder if instead of bending, he's broken, had a heart attack over at the allotment, is lying slumped facedown in his plot. That thought makes me pick the receiver up, put it to my ear.

I say hello, but no one answers. I repeat it and the caller maintains their silence. A third time, the same result, and I disconnect the call and place the phone back on the charger. I really couldn't say why I'm so convinced it's her, but I am; Sweetie Nelson, the only connection between Ryan and Tyson Manley. It was her I saw this morning and she is the person ringing me now, holding on without saying a word, I'm sure of it.

I run a bath and leave the door to Ryan's room slightly ajar for Sheba to come and go as she pleases. I take valerian, two capsules, to help me sleep. I pour a glass of vodka and cranberry, a big one, light on the mixer, knock it back as I lie in the bath. It is almost ten by the time I get into bed and turn off the light. About twenty minutes later, I hear keys in the front door, know Lloydie has arrived back home. He does what he has been doing for the last seven months; stays downstairs with the TV on till he thinks I have fallen asleep.

There has been no intimacy since Ryan died, and part of me is glad because I don't know how to feel joy in my son's absence, cannot imagine how to kiss and be touched, feel thrill with the pleasure rise, no longer know if I am entitled or have a right. But Lloydie was never a talker, never really demonstrative outside of our bed. That was the place our disagreements were concluded, the only time he felt able to put aside his role as provider and supporter, husband and father, the only place he allowed me to see his vulnerability, the strong man who never hurt me once, even the first time, who sometimes cried when he came. The absence of that intimacy is not just an absence of the physical act, it is an absence of the emotional bond we shared. I lie with my eyes open and listen to him and the effect is like the sound of a sad song. If there is a route to rediscovering our middle ground I do not know the way.

Despite the valerian-vodka cocktail, I'm still awake an hour later, but when I hear Lloydie sneaking into our room, putting on his PJs as quietly as he can in the dark, I feign sleep. I do not move when I feel him slipping into the bed, careful not to touch or wake me. It is only when he turns his back to mine that I realize I am already crying.

3

THE NOISE OF THE SHOWER wakes me. My head feels groggy, maybe because I had the two valerian capsules or too much vodka, or both. It feels early, but a glance at the clock radio tells me it is nearly nine thirty. I open the drawer beneath it, dig out the packet of paracetamol, and take two with water from the bottle permanently on the side. My routine morning assessment; this is a bad day. I close my eyes again, put my head back down. After the funeral, Lorna insisted I get my doctor to refer me to a bereavement counselor; in fact, she said we should both go, Lloydie and I, but he wouldn't. Lorna was right, it was exactly what I needed; Jenny, her name was, such a lovely woman, with the eyes you would expect of someone who does such a job and does it well, brimful with empathy. I was furious with everyone at the time. My grief had made me fixated on blame, apportioning it as if it made any difference to what had happened. Tiny details were exaggerated in my mind till I was filled with rage for everyone including Lloydie, because of those boots. She helped me to get things in perspective. Seeing her then probably saved my marriage, such as it is.

One of the things that came out of it was my strategy for dealing with days like this; don't expect too much from yourself. Itemize what needs to be done and tackle them one by one. Complete each thing in order before moving on to the next. Keep your list short. If I cannot make myself begin, my day will be spent here in bed. It is a hard desire to fight but I will, not because I have anything specific to do, but because I know from experience that the longer I lie here and do nothing, the longer it will take me to find the strength to get up. If I do not force myself to get moving, I could be lying in my bed for days. Mentally, I make my list.

I will only lie here till Lloydie comes out of the bathroom and back into this room.

When he does, I'll ask if he intends to come to court at all, or if he is just planning on sticking his head in the sand for the whole trial.

I will accept whatever answer he gives me then get up, brush my teeth, and have my shower.

I will get dressed and comb my hair—ha-ha.

I'll drink my tea.

This is doable.

Except Lloydie doesn't come back into the bedroom. I realize at some point that the paracetamol is kicking in and that it has been some time since the shower stopped running. Eighteen years and I know my husband's habits as well as I know my own. He has his shower, comes out, sits on the edge of his side of the bed with his towel underneath him, and creams himself before putting on his deodorant and getting dressed. I even know the order in which he gets dressed. His boxers are first, then the socks, followed by his vest, his trousers, and his top last of all. When I hear the sound of a canister hissing I know he has taken the day's attire and all his toiletries into the bathroom with him. I wonder if he will be forced to return to collect his shoes from under the bed, but when he unlocks the door, I hear him crossing the hallway to the stairs and, from the sound, know his shoes are already on his feet.

I get up. I push my own feet into the slippers under my side of the bed and tie my dressing gown tightly around my waist. If he will not come to the bedroom, I will speak to him downstairs. I am halfway down when the doorbell rings. I retreat to the landing as Lloydie opens the front door and I hear familiar voices, Pastor Meade from the church at the top of our road and a couple of the sisters from his church who have been fairly regular visitors since the event, have given us much support. It is another of the things that have changed in our lives, the public forum our world has become. Really, truly, it is wonderful to know others are thinking of us, to know of all the people out there who want to help in some way, to be there for us, but sometimes it feels as though I have no privacy anymore, no longer an entitlement to choose who I spend my time with, where and for how long. Some days, like today, it's not condolences and sympathy I want, I just want to be allowed to do what I feel like, to stay in my jammies all day if I wish, to lie on Ryan's bed, to speak to my husband about what remains of our marriage and the commitment he made to me.

As Lloydie invites them in, I tiptoe back across the landing to our bedroom. He doesn't have a religious bone in his body but he's happy to fill our home with anything that means he and I will not be alone or in a situation where there is the opportunity to properly talk. He has taken them into the kitchen. I hear the sounds of chairs scraping the floor, them settling in. I pick up the phone and call Lorna's landline. There is no answer. I ring her mobile, hoping she has maybe only just left and I'm not too late to go with her to Nottingham. Her mobile goes straight to voice mail. She's probably already zooming down the M1 motorway. I leave a message for her to give Leah a hug and kiss for me. Then I grab my towel and go to have my shower.

Lloydie is putting my cup of tea on the side when I return to the bedroom. He looks slightly sheepish, is probably annoyed with himself for the mistiming that has meant he has found himself alone with me when we are both awake and alert. He looks at me without speaking.

"Aren't you gonna ask how it went?" I ask.

It's not the question I intended, too in your face, accusatory. I didn't want to start the discussion here but it's out now, I can't take it back.

His tone is dutiful. "How did it go?"

"It was hard. Listening. Seeing that boy, his mother. Very hard."

He sits down on the bed, bows his head, and cups his face with his hands. His hair hasn't fallen out. It is as full as it has ever been, but the last seven months have bleached it near white. If he didn't care, if he were unaffected, it might have made my response to him less complicated. Instead I know how impossibly hard this is for him. I know he blames himself and how much of that is down to me. But my empathy is matched by my anger, which wants to insist on more from him yet is frustrated by his fragility, the acute sense of attacking a helpless creature, which in turn fuels the rage that I have been made to be wrong in this, wrong to expect anything at this time from my husband; *my husband!*

"I don't get it," I say. "What the plan is. Are you just gonna dodge me and hide till this is all over?"

"Over?" he asks. "It's already over."

"So the boy who killed him, you don't think he needs to pay?"

"What difference does it make?"

He's talking about Ryan and he's right; this trial won't bring him back, but should we all down tools, find a corner somewhere to sit and hold our heads?

"You should want to come."

He says, "I can't do it, none of this, I can't."

"But I can? You can't, but by some magic it's all a doddle for me? The strength just appears to me miraculously? You can just opt out and leave me to deal with this stinking shitty broken mess on my own?"

He doesn't answer. My voice has risen, is too loud, bordering hysterical. There are people downstairs. I sit at the dressing table, take the towel off my head, open the hair grease, rub a small amount between my palms then on my head, and look at myself in the mirror. I hardly recognize my reflection, hardly know who this person is, this balding screaming banshee; hardly recognize the people we've become.

He used to kiss and cuddle Ryan when he was a baby, but he started pulling back from physical affection almost in proportion to the rate at which our son grew, not because he did not love him, but because he did; he loved our son as much as I did, still does. But the image of fatherhood in Lloydie's mind is without words or caresses. It is a silent movie where he can be seen repairing Ryan's bed frame, leaving pocket and dinner money on the edge of the kitchen table daily, tightening the brakes on his bicycle, checking the air in its tires. I know this about him, have always known it. But I gave Ryan enough of the soft things, enough openly demonstrative love to compensate for spaces where there would otherwise have been a lack. I never pressured Lloydie to dig deeper within himself, and it is probably one of the reasons our marriage worked, because Lloydie has no reserves to dig into, they simply don't exist. Our son's death has left him completely emotionally crippled. Unlike me, discovering internal resources I never imagined from the depths of my being, he can't deal with any of this. He's not lying.

"Those people downstairs, I don't want to talk to them. I'm getting dressed, then I'm going out."

He doesn't look up. "Okay."

"Will you be here when I get back?"

"Was gonna go to the allotment . . . I don't know."

"Then I'll see you later . . . maybe."

He finally releases his head and stands. "Okay."

I wear a scarf on my head when I go out, drift down to the market, wander through the peopled space from stall to stall. It strikes me again just how many beautiful black boys there are in the world, how little I noticed of life with my old eyes. They saunter past me beatboxing aloud, wait outside butchers' shops beside trolley bags for their mums, are leaning against shopfronts or cavorting on the green, showing off and at the same time pretending not to notice the girls. They distract me, these young boys, cocoa-, demerara-, and vanilla-skinned, small and tall, confident and awkward, with skiffles and afros and cornrows and futures, years filled with football and Wii, jerk chicken and study, hours spent peering into mirrors and carrying out the meticulous investigation of new baby hair on cheeks and chin. There are so many of them, so strong and dark and beautiful, alive everywhere, and their presence occupies me like an obsessive-compulsive disorder that breaks the heart.

When I leave the market it is without having bought anything, more of a resignation than an ending. The weather is holding up and so I walk in the direction of the park. The high street is busy with Saturday shopping traffic, the roads and pavements and bus stops are heaving. I stop at the corner of a block where it is possible to jaywalk rather than walk to the lights that you're meant to use to cross this busy road safely, notice once again that it is the perfect spot to die.

I wait there, watching the buses as they leave the stop about two hundred meters up the street. The traffic lights are another hundred meters past where I am standing. There are no zebra crossings or humps or reasons for a busy bus to slow and so they always pick up speed along this stretch. When Ryan was young, I read that a jeep traveling at thirty miles an hour that hits a child will almost certainly kill him. It stands to reason a bus maybe ten times that weight traveling at a similar speed is enough to kill an adult. I watch the bus that is at the stop fill with the queuing passengers and their shopping and bags, close its doors. It departs slowly, pulls from the curbside to the center, begins picking up speed. Precision timing is the key to ensuring the only life you take is your own. A person who stepped out too early would be seen by the driver, who might attempt to steer around them, possibly crash in the process, and others might die. There is a point about five meters away at which, if the driver has his foot down, you could simply step off the curb in front of the bus and be instantly killed. I can see it is traveling fast enough already. As it gets closer, I begin to make out the features on the driver's face. It is almost at the perfect spot . . . nearly there . . .

I am stunned to feel the top of my arm being pulled, to hear the blare of the bus horn, to feel the gust of turbulence as the bus passes me, raising a whirlwind of street dust in its wake, and turn around to face a woman who isn't familiar, staring at me, scared.

"You okay?" she asks.

I blink furiously, wipe my left eye, can feel grit in it. My heart is pounding. I collect myself and nod. "Yes."

She says, "You're the mother, aren't you?"

"Sorry?"

"Of that boy who got stabbed. The one who died. I read about it in the papers when it happened. It's terrible. My sons go to the same school. I don't know what I'd do if anything happened to them."

She lied; she does know. She didn't just recognize me, she also saw the trail of my thinking. She knows too well what she might be moved to do, but lucky her, it wasn't her sons, it was mine. I don't want to discuss this, so I simply wait in the hope she'll move on.

"Are you sure you're okay?" she asks again. She doesn't want to leave me here, will not go.

"Yes," I say and walk away. I hate unnecessary rudeness, and I'm acutely aware of just how rude I'm being, but I cannot talk to her, cannot talk about it. I walk away quickly in the general direction of the park.

I buy myself a cookie and a coffee from the café near the park entrance and go inside. I find a bench close to the swings, take a seat, observe the children playing, and listen to them laugh. I watch the mothers more critically than I ever did before, upset when they exhibit the same impatience I exhibited when my Ryan was young enough to be taken to the swings and old enough to be uncooperative.

That woman on the high street asked me if I was "the mother." I don't think I am. The second Sunday after Ryan was taken was Mother's Day, and I don't know how I got through it, can hardly bear to think about the next. If it was possible to die of grief it would have happened that day. The worst part was trying to work out whether in addition to losing my son, I had lost my "mother" status, didn't know whether I still qualified, was unable to satisfy myself or be satisfied by the responses from Lorna and Leah and the masses of people who visited to help me make it through that wretched day. In the end I looked it up in the dictionary, found the definition. It said that "mother" is the relationship of a woman to her child. I have three dictionaries at home and I looked it up in each of them. None of them explained whether that status was rescinded if there was no longer a child for such a woman to have a relationship with. So am I a mother? I don't think I am, but it is too complicated to explain to every person I meet, too loaded and depressing. When people ask if I'm okay, it is exactly what they do *not* want me to elaborate on, another issue I cannot discuss, one more thing to swallow and hold down.

It is ironic there is so much I can no longer talk about when inside I am filled with speeches. I want to get up and talk to those impatient mums, want them to know how fragile is the gift of children that has been given them, how easily and irrevocably they can be taken, how precious every moment is, every second and hour and day, the infinite joy in their possession already, the exact value of which can only be precisely measured in its dearth. I want to teach them to rejoice that they have no difficulty answering when someone asks as simple a question as "You're the mother, aren't you?" But of course, I don't. I just watch them and sip my coffee and eat my cookie. And I listen to the laughter and occasional cries.

From where I am sitting I can see the blocks of social housing where Tyson Manley's mother lives, where he lived before he was in prison, really just a half-hour stroll from my home; a group of quick-build low-cost boxes, a Lego town occupying the ground between the entrance to the railway station and an imposing block of luxury apartments with floor-to-ceiling windows and huge balconies from where the view is no doubt spectacular, overlooking the park. There are places in the world I would never travel to, war zones where people live in daily fear for their lives, where families are all too familiar with violent death, the random bloody loss of those they love. They are the parts of the world I have never visited because I didn't want to face that kind of danger, the risks were too high. Instead I lived here in the UK, bought a cozy house in a quiet street and satisfied myself for years that I was lucky for it, and all the while looked sympathetically at charity adverts or snippets on the news of those victims of warring and genocide, and felt sympathy, as if I with my safe life in this safe land were exempted from it, truly believed we were.

The sun has gone behind the clouds, my hot coffee is now cold and the air chilly. I get up and begin to walk toward the estate. I don't know why. Perhaps to see whether I enter something like a scene from a Hollywood action film, gangsters on the corners and armed police with loudspeakers shouting, "Put your weapons down!" It is nothing like that. It must be about one now and the estate is quiet, peaceful even. The homes are a bit worn, slightly dilapidated; the railings and doors and windows could be improved with a fresh lick of paint. There is some graffiti, but it is not excessive, play equipment that looks like it's been in place for two decades, green areas gone brown. It's not perfect, but I've seen worse. I work out which house the Manleys occupy and I walk past it slowly, just looking. Their address was in a document I saw long before we went to court, had not been redacted on a report from social services, and it always surprised me, the close proximity of their home to mine, like the scene from *The Godfather* where a man wakes to find a horse's head in his bed, way too close for comfort.

The Manleys have an iron gate fitted over the front door, grilles on the windows downstairs. I look around and notice that almost all of the houses on the estate have these, and at once it makes the environment more sinister, more like the kind of place where special provisions need to be made to keep your family safe. The front gardens are tiny fenced areas, more of a container than an outdoor space, just about big enough for a wheelie bin and a recycling box. The recycling box outside the Manleys' is a black crate on the ground to the right of the door. It is almost full. I can see beer and empty cans inside it, newspapers neatly folded, an empty brandy bottle, carrier bags, the plastic packaging of frozen vegetables and oven chips, and I am stunned.

I continue to the end of the estate, turn around and walk back, check again, notice an empty toilet roll tube and some used tinfoil I didn't spot on my first pass. I walk back to and through the park and try to understand it, the notion that Ms. Manley would be concerned about recycling, that she would be actively trying to improve her carbon footprint, reduce energy, that she would wash out and set aside her empty glass bottles to reduce unnecessary waste going to landfill sites, that the mother of at least one son who kills people would go to the trouble of collecting and neatly folding the daily papers, conscientiously disposing of them, doing her part to save trees, protect habitats and endangered species. The logic of it defies me.

When I get home I find Lloydie has left and those visitors are gone. Though it is still fairly early, I make myself a vodka, drink it, pour another, sip the second one more slowly. I do not want people around me, yet my life is so full of space I hardly know how to fill it. I want something to do, to discover Ryan's mess somewhere. I want to find the milk for his cereal boiled over onto the plate inside the microwave, solid lumps of toothpaste cemented to the bathroom sink. I want my son, not just those moments that were so glorious but all of it, the upsets and frustrations and angst, everything that came as part and parcel of being his mother, his being alive. It is an impossible wish, and so I go to his room.

Sheba is already in there, curled up on the center of the bed. She looks up at me when I enter, is unimpressed, puts her head back down again, and drifts off. It is bright enough outside to see but still I draw my son's curtains, inhaling deeply while I do it because Ryan's room is losing his scent. At some point it will be completely gone and this room will smell exactly like what it is; unoccupied. For the time being, however, I can still raise faint traces of the old smell through a couple of means, one of which is drawing the curtains, shifting them so they trap a pocket of air and billow. It is really hard to describe how I feel as I inhale and catch that scent. It is purely emotional and concentrated in the heart. There is a sweet sharp joy, piercing, exquisite. In equal measure there is an excruciating sadness that is physical, like the pain behind the eyes when you stare directly into the sun. The moment lasts a few seconds only, two or three at the most, then is gone.

I turn on Ryan's bedside lamp. It casts a feeble circle of light a meter in diameter against the darkness. I lie on his bed carefully, arranging myself around Sheba as he did, so she is not disturbed. I lie on my side facing her, put my hand onto her soft warm back, and stroke. She unfurls beneath my fingers lazily, tries to rub the side of her face against my hand, purring like a diesel engine. She was always Ryan's cat, slept in here with him every night. Ryan wasn't a tough guy, a macho man in the making, he was soft and gentle and feely. Wherever he was in the house, Sheba would invariably be close by because she was guaranteed his time, attention, and affection. Even though he is no longer here, she still sleeps in his room, and sometimes I think she is the only living creature who remembers him with the same intensity that I do.

There was a day, about a fortnight after the event, when I had some laundry on the kitchen floor that I had finally sorted into piles after weeks of inactivity. I had run out of soap powder and walked to the corner shop to pick up some more. When I returned, Sheba was lying on one of the piles of washing. There was a pair of Ryan's boxer shorts in that pile and she was rubbing the side of her face into the crotch and purring as blissfully as if it were catnip. I just sat down on the floor beside her and cried as I watched. I could understand it so completely, the way his absence amplified her need to connect with him, even if it was only through inhaling his scent; in fact, I was jealous. Propriety stopped me, but I wanted to do it too, lie on the floor, push her out of the way, rub my face into his pants in her place, deeply inhale.

Those were mad weeks. All I could think about was connecting with him. I read his schoolbooks, every word of every essay and answer and sentence he wrote, searching for his essence. I listened to the same boog-a-boog house music I'd spent years asking him to turn down, *please!* I watched the programs he'd loved that I had told him were polluting his mind, spent time in his room, sat at his desk, lay on his bed, pored over his image in photographs. I even went up into the attic, brought down boxes of memorabilia; an envelope containing every baby tooth he ever lost, bar one which he swallowed accidentally and cried because he worried his carelessness had cost him the hard cash the tooth fairy would have left for it (it didn't, still earned him in its absence two pounds); fingered the blue baby band placed on his wrist within an hour of birth, the wretched dried stump of his umbilical cord and peg, all the things I had collected that I imagined I would one day present to him, maybe when he was twenty-one or when he had a child of his own, or that he might discover in the attic after I had died, never dreamed I would need these worthless precious items so badly, that they would be all I had left of him, all I had left, otherwise I would have collected more, videoed every moment, recorded every word, bubble-wrapped every item he ever touched if

I'd thought for a second that he would be taken from me so early and they would be all I'd have to console me for the rest of my life.

I want my son. Want him so badly it hurts. Remembering him is not enough. Being in his room is not enough. Catching his scent is not enough. I want my son.

Lloydie returns earlier than he did last night and cooks. It is easier to eat the dinner he has prepared on trays on our laps in the living room rather than at the kitchen table, so we can both stare at the TV screen as though deeply immersed, taking the pressure off the silence between us and creating the appearance of being a normal married couple spending a regular evening at home.

I am angry with myself for wanting more from Lloydie, not because it is unreasonable to want more from him under the circumstances, but because my expectations are unfair. He cannot speak of feelings, never has been able to. It's part of his psyche. His father was a hard man, brutal with Lloydie and his sister. Their mother died when he was six and he grew up with a man who clothed and fed and disciplined them, nothing more. He never had a mother cuddle him when he was ten or twelve or twenty, never spoke while he was growing up with his father about feelings or emotions or life. One of the first things he told me when we were courting was that when he had children he intended to be better than his father was, that he would never lay a hand on them in anger, and he never did. He threw out those things from his own upbringing that were the worst and unacceptable, but he didn't replace them with positives, maybe he didn't know how, and I always accepted it, accepted every shortcoming for better or worse.

How he is sitting here this evening is how he would have sat here eating dinner a year ago. What made the difference was that Ryan and I would have filled the silence. This barrier is not of his making, it is mine; I'm the one who has changed. Impotence has closed down the one channel of emotional communication that was open to him before, and that he cannot communicate with me and cannot cope with listening to me talk about Ryan, when the only thing I want to talk about is Ryan, has meant I have stopped communicating as well. But how can I? How do I talk about those things that mean nothing to me? What do I do with all the other words stuck in my throat, my stomach, my heart? How do I ignore or simply bypass them?

I leave him downstairs afterward to watch TV on his own till he thinks I've fallen asleep, go up to my bedroom, and phone my sister. She is back home now and fills me in with the details of her day, the seven-bedroom student flat my niece now shares, the disaster of Leah's first attempts to cook unsupervised, the breadth of the campus, the drama of its autumn landscape, its beauty, how safe it makes you feel when you are there, and I love her for this as I listen to the subtext, know she is trying to reduce my anxieties, to allay my neuroses around rapists and killers and people who slip into the world of those you love most when least expected, to destroy everything you thought you had with but a thrust. I tell her to come tomorrow and have dinner with me and Lloydie, and she reminds me about tomorrow afternoon's Family Day. I had completely forgotten about it. She asks if Lloydie is going with me.

"I told him about it weeks ago," I say. "He hasn't mentioned it. He's probably forgot."

"You should try to convince him to go with you. It'd be good for him."

There is much that would be good for him, but he's just not interested in any of it. I say, "I'll try."

"I'm gonna be here," she says. "Phone me if he's not going and I'll come with you."

I say, "Okay. Thanks."

"But try him first. Try your best to convince him."

I say, "I will."

"Don't go in all guns blazing. Be gentle with him, okay?"

I say, "Okay."

I wake up when Lloydie turns the shower on, drift back off, and wake again when he comes out and goes downstairs. Once again he must have taken everything with him to the bathroom to avoid returning, being here alone with me in our room, yet another new routine to chip away at the supporting foundations of our marriage. A few more and it will be impossible to distinguish what remains of us two beyond the rising cloud of dust.

I remember the Family Day. It is an event organized by a charity that works with people who have lost someone close to violence. It was Nipa who put me in contact with them. I want to go to it, want us both to go, but I know he will be reluctant. I need to time it perfectly, warm him up in advance. I begin by smiling at him when he brings me my cup of tea. He says he's popping out to the supermarket for some bits for us and also Rose and Dan. I say if he'll wait, I'll go with him. I can see he is surprised. He agrees to wait. I have a wash and get ready quickly. He's standing by the front door with his coat on by the time I get downstairs.

We take the bus to the supermarket, passing our car, parked outside the house in the same spot it's been in for months. Despite my sister's advice that every woman should be able to drive, I've never learned, was happy to be dropped off and collected, and Lloydie was happy to add the chauffeuring around of me and Ryan to the job description of husband and father that he has always kept in his head. But he can't drive now, like he can't talk or come to court or go to work. He's been on sick leave from his job as an estate manager for over six months now. He can't concentrate for long on single tasks, except those that can be carried out on autopilot or involve his allotment. I think the best thing he could do for himself is to go back, bring some structure to his day, force himself into everyday discussions and conversations, begin the process of normalizing his life again, but he won't. He has opted out of every part of the life he had before, and unless something inside him shifts, unless something happens to make him want to, he will remain as stagnant as the Audi sitting on the curbside outside our home, lacking purpose.

There was an incident one day when he nearly knocked down a child on a zebra crossing. That's how he tells it, as if the incident involved emergency braking, wild swerving, the black burn of locked wheels across the tarmac, a hairline miss. But he didn't so much nearly knock her down as simply fail to notice her patiently waiting to cross. He didn't see her till he was on the crossing itself driving past. How many drivers have had similar experiences and are still in their cars on the road? Probably all of them. But in Lloydie's mind, this single event has come to symbolize the danger to society he represents behind the wheel, so he no longer drives. He washes it though, polishes it regularly, and vacuums the inside. He makes sure the tax disc and insurance are up to date. He went down last month from half pay to statutory sick pay. If he does not return to work before his SSP runs out, when money gets even tighter, that car will be the first thing to be sold.

We pass the car and catch the bus, and it is a bit like watching TV together over dinner, each of us staring with fascination through the window as the bus drives through streets we know as intimately as the backs of our hands, and I try to find the words to gently remind him about the Family Day, and fail. The supermarket is much easier. We speak of the things we need, quantities and brands and prices. We talk about how expensive staple items are, the disconnectedness of our government with the people, especially those who have the least and need help the most. We act our parts to perfection, just a regular married couple doing the usual things they do. The conversation winds down after we have paid, comes to an end by the time we board the bus to take us back home.

I help him unpack the bags, separating out the things that need to go next door. Almost the entire morning has passed without my saying a word. This is ridiculous. How bad have things gotten that it should be such a struggle to simply speak?

Finally, I go for it. "Have you remembered about the Family Day?" I ask. "It's this afternoon. I want to go. I really want you to come with me."

He says, "You go. It's not my kinda thing."

"You don't have to speak to anyone. Just be with me. That's all."

"It's not for me."

"You're not doing anything to help yourself."

"I don't need that kinda help."

I am remembering my sister's words of advice, to go in gently, but it doesn't help. I hear myself shout, "What *do* you need, Lloyd? 'Cause I don't know anymore. What is it? Me? Do you even need me?"

He doesn't answer, won't now that I've shouted. Instead he continues unpacking the shopping without looking at me, moving more slowly, hoping, I'm sure, to drag the job out till the conversation's done. And I should stop, I know this clearly, I should back off now, but I can't. I snatch the bag from his hands, hurl it across the room, hear the cans inside it spill out and roll across the floor as I screech, "Are you still my husband or not?"

Still there is no answer. Maybe that's a good thing. He isn't coming and nothing he can say to me is going to make me feel any better about it. He is collecting the cans from the floor as I leave the kitchen, go upstairs, and phone my sister.

I'm not sure quite what I was expecting of the Family Day, only that when we enter the community center hall and I look around, I know it wasn't this. There are French windows running the length of one wall, opening up onto the grounds outside where there are children playing, shrieking and hanging from a climbing frame, screaming and soaring across a bouncy castle. There is a barbeque going, people queuing for food, people and buggies gathered around a seating area beside it; families having fun. Inside, the hall is packed, a large space filled with activities; a table at which adults and children sit making chimes, a corner where head-and-shoulder massages are being carried out, a canteen area where there are cakes and cookies, tea and coffee. There is hair braiding, a henna stall, manicures being carried out at the table beside it, a long slow queue of children patiently waiting for their faces to be painted. Perhaps it was a more somber event I was expecting, something along the lines of a memorial service. This event has the ambience of a fair.

A woman with a kind face comes over, introduces herself as June, the woman who runs the charity. She tells us to relax, have a wander, meet some of the other families, asks if we brought along a photograph of Ryan, suggests we begin by adding it to the board. The board is exactly what it sounds like and occupies a corner of the room with eight chairs in two rows in front of it like pews. This quiet corner is closer to how I imagined the event would be. There are lit candles on one side of the board, a tall and beautiful vase of elegant flowers on the other. Pinned to it are photographs, so many of them, and so many of the subjects so young and full of life. In the entrance hall at Ryan's school, his old school, there was a wall filled with hundreds of pictures of pupils and staff. I loved the energy of it, all those faces covering that space, the immediate recognition you were in a place concerned with people, children, life. Standing here, the energy is completely different; sad and also shocking. I take my time, move my eyes across the images slowly, consciously examining each face, trying to feel the people they were from the images that are all that remains of them, so many people—how many? thirty-five? forty?—all these healthy happy people smiling for the cameras, posing, every single one of them wiped from the face of this earth, violently. It is the sum of all these images assembled here together in one place that is shocking. What I am looking at is sad and shocking and something else besides that I feel but cannot identify or articulate.

Lorna says, "I'm gonna get a cup of tea, you want one?"

"Please."

"You gonna come with me?"

I say, "I'll wait here."

She goes off and I stand there, still trying to understand my feelings. It is sadness and it is shock and it is something else that is uplifting, and that puzzles me.

"Which one's yours?" a woman asks. I look up at her, older than I am, early to mid-fifties perhaps, of African descent, tall and dark and slim. I point to Ryan's photo. "Your son?" she asks.

"Yes."

"He is handsome. What is his name?"

"Ryan. Which one's yours?"

She points to a picture of a boy who looks even younger than Ryan, maybe fourteen or fifteen, all teeth and exuberance, grinning into the camera.

"I love his eyes. They look full of mischief," I say.

She laughs, a proper laugh, full, deeply tickled. "Ahh, Patrice, he was full of mischief, ach, used to drive me mad, always up to something, used to make me laugh, that boy."

"When did he die?" I ask.

"In December will be eight years. And you?"

Not *when did he die?* but *when did this happen to you?* "Nearly eight months ago."

"This time is hard, but it will get better. You do not think it can but it will. Believe me, I know."

"Thank you for that," I say, and I mean those thanks

with a depth of emotion that makes me tearful. And suddenly I am able to identify that positive feeling. Since Ryan's death, I have heard every uttering of sympathy, every cliché, been told by so many people that they know what I'm going through, that life goes on, time is the great healer, that in fact there are things to be thankful for; that my son was not suffering illness, his was a quick death instead of a painful one dragged out slowly over time. Lloydie's father came to visit us after Lloydie phoned and told him. It was always going to be a difficult visit anyway because he had so little to do with his grandson throughout his too short life, never really got to know him or spend time with him, but he came as people do when something this tragic occurs, a visit dictated by protocol, and he said, which I will never forgive him for, how lucky I was to be young enough to have another, as if Ryan was nothing more than a car or a winter coat or a boiler. I was too devastated by his insensitivity to reply, but I have replied to others and sometimes thanked them, while at the same time rejecting their condolences and sympathy because, actually, they haven't a clue. This is the first time I have met someone who has lost a child through violence, who has experienced what I have experienced, who has been through what I am going through, who has truly, genuinely felt it. It is the first time in seven months that I have not felt isolated because of my experience, but part of something, in the same way that the photo of Ryan on the board has gone from representing an individual loss to forming part of a collective issue.

I know there is violence in this country. I've seen it on the news and *Crime Watch*. I've read the papers, the stories about people being stabbed, gunned down, women killed by spouses, children at the hands of the parents who were supposed to protect them, but it has always been a story in isolation, neatly wrapped up before moving on to the next news item. Here, I am surrounded by all these people, sixty, maybe seventy of them, and each one, including the people who run the charity, the guy who's doing the barbeque, the masseur, the woman making the teas, every one of us shares this bloody reality so easily dismissed by outsiders as an aberration, called "isolated incidents" by the media and the police, all these people, of different colors and origins and religions and none, middle and lower and upper class, as diverse a group of people as you're likely to meet anywhere, all together, all bereaved, all coping with hideous grief in our own way. It is the most engaged I've felt at any event since Ryan passed.

I introduce myself to Patrice's mother, learn her name is Fimi, introduce her to Lorna when she returns with the teas, discover her son, like mine, was also a fatal teenage stabbing victim. Apparently he gave the wrong boy a look that was interpreted as disrespect—a look, her son died because of a look—his murderer another young boy, fifteen years at the time, still incarcerated today, eight years on; two more young lives wasted. I feel myself studying Fimi as she speaks and I know what I am seeking. It is there behind her eyes, the grief, but she has pulled through. I want to know how she did it, where she found the strength and how she harnessed it, how anyone harnesses enough strength in this circumstance to keep going, not just to remain alive, but to live.

A little girl runs over to us, pretty and pigtailed, about six,

Fimi's daughter, followed almost immediately by her father, panicking because she was out of his sight for a few moments; their consequent child. As soon as her interest is caught, the daughter skips off with her father in close and watchful pursuit. Fimi joins Lorna and me as we drink our teas, then introduces us to some of the other attendees, whom she has met at similar events in the past.

I talk about Ryan to the woman who lost her husband in a robbery gone too far, to the mother of a daughter killed by the man she didn't want to go out with, a man whose son was simply in the wrong place at the wrong time, caught in the crossfire between two gangs in a shoot-out that sounds more like a scene from a western than urban Britain. I talk about my son and I listen to them talk about those people they have lost, and the things they have gone on to do after; marathons to raise funds to do good, charities to save potential victims or give comfort to survivors like me, and I am filled with too many emotions to keep track of. I could cry for every person here, all those photographs, the people they represent, for the avoidable, unnecessary pain, the waste. Yet I am elated to be here amongst others who understand the need to remember, to talk about their loved ones, who understand how vital it is to listen—people like me. More than anything I wish Lloydie had come along with me, that he had been part of this.

The day ends at seven, after dusk, with the release of Chinese lanterns into the sky, one for every person here, in memory of those who have brought us all together, and for a short while the night sky is illuminated by a constellation of flickering lights. I wait and watch till the glow from the final lantern is extinguished, can feel an emotional exhaustion descend upon me as I do the rounds with Lorna before leaving, taking numbers, saying goodbye.

"Thanks for coming with me," I say to Lorna, when she pulls up outside my home. The house is in darkness. Lloydie is not inside.

"It was good for me as well. I'm really glad I came. Out now. Get some sleep. We've got a big day ahead."

"I'll see you in the morning," I say as I step onto the pavement.

She says, "Bye. Sweet dreams," before I close the car door and she drives away.

4

THE ALARM AWAKENS ME ABRUPTLY, severs me from my dream of Ryan dying, the first one from which I have woken wishing it had continued. I turn the alarm off and quickly lie back down and close my eyes in the hope of returning to it, but it doesn't happen. After enough time has passed for me to accept that, I carry out my regular morning assessment; this is a manageable day, on the scale, maybe even good. I will be able to get up without struggle, get ready and over to the court-room, where I can sit and watch that boy for the entire day. I drink the tea on the side, stroke Sheba, and relive the dream. When I finally look at the clock, I am flabbergasted to discover so much time has passed so quickly, and I go from being as relaxed as I can remember in a long while into a panic, begin a mad dash to get showered and dressed and ready before Nipa arrives. I hear her ring the doorbell, and as I go down the stairs to let her in, the phone rings. I pick up the receiver in the hallway. As soon as she says "Hello," I know who it is.

She says, "I need to talk to you."

"Why are you calling me?"

"I just wanna talk . . ."

"Sweetie, I'm at court today, I'm sure you know that."

"I know you must hate me. If I have to beg, I will, but you've gotta meet me."

"Look, I haven't got time for this right now. You know where my house is . . ."

"I can't come to your house. You don't know, man, there's people clocking everything I do. It's gotta be outta the area."

"You'll have to give me your number. I'll phone you back later . . ."

"You can't call me. Look, my money's gonna run out. There's a café, at the top of the market, Hulya's. Meet me there tonight at six thirty. You have to. . . ."

Then nothing. I say, "Hello? Hello?" The line goes dead.

This is bloody ridiculous. I put the phone down, go and answer the door, tell Nipa I'll be just a minute, lock up, and leave. I don't mention the call to Nipa, am not sure I should even be speaking to Sweetie, don't know whether just that phone call has already meant I've broken rules, wonder about the wisdom of meeting with her at all, why I didn't do what I should've done, said no then put the phone down, but that only lasts a moment. There is no great mystery underlying my desire to meet with her. It is the same force that drives me to get up and attend this trial; I want to understand why my son is dead. She is the single link between Ryan and Tyson Manley. She knows why this has happened. She hasn't told the police, but if I meet with her, maybe she'll tell me.

There is so much I wish were different, so many things I wish I could turn the clock back and change, and high up on my list is the wish that Sweetie and my son had never met. When I get into the car, I tell Nipa about my day yesterday, and when I finish, we drive in silence, and my mind is filled with thoughts of that girl.

He'd been acting strangely for weeks, humming more, happier than usual. Getting ready already took him ages anyway, but it was taking even longer; brushing and smoothing his hair and eyebrows, trying out Lloydie's aftershaves, sneaking splashes of the most expensive brands. I watched him like I had been watching him since he was a baby, with the interest I always had when he was learning or embarked on something new, from swimming to speaking French. I never knew where it came from, his innate capacity to master new things, his fearless ability to venture into the unknown and emerge triumphant, thought it was one of the miraculous blessings of nature, his love of life and everything in it, and when he finally brought it up before he left the house for school, it was as casually as if he were asking for money for lunch, or reminding me he was going to the cinema in the evening with his mates.

"I was gonna bring a friend home later . . ."

"A friend?"

"To do some revision, for English."

"Okay."

"She's a girl."

"A girl?"

"Uh-huh."

"Er . . . I think we're gonna need some rules."

"That's *just* what I was thinking," Ryan said, laughing.

"I'm not joking," I said, smiling nonetheless. "You both stay downstairs at all times . . ."

"But I wanted to show her the view from my window."

"And she needs to go home at a respectable time . . ."

"Aww, I was hoping she could sleep over."

"And no funny business."

"Are we talking about sexual intercourse?"

"*Ryan!*"

"Mum, we're revising English, not biology."

"I'm serious," I said.

"I know. Deal," he said, still laughing, and kissed me as he slung his schoolbag up onto his back and walked out of the kitchen toward the front door. He had just opened it when I shouted, "What's her name?" Then I heard it close. If he was bringing a girl home, I assumed this must be serious. If it was a milestone for him, it was an even bigger one for me as a parent. I had already had conversations with him sporadically, naturally arising from the circumstances we found ourselves in, about not treating women like the objects they are portrayed as in music videos, celebrity magazines, and porn; about mutual respect, consensual sex, contraception, and sexually transmitted diseases; but they had always been abstract, laying the groundwork for his future relationships. I had been determined to never be one of those parents who buried their head in the sand, who had important conversations in the form of a cussing after things had gone wrong and it was already too late. This development meant some more specific conversations needed to be had, and quickly.

They were in the kitchen when I came in from work. I had left slightly earlier than usual. I'm not suggesting I had a genuine concern that if I arrived back at my normal time, by then I'd be well on the road to becoming a grandma, but Ryan bringing home his first girlfriend had been on my mind for pretty much the entire day.

When I opened the front door, I heard them both laughing in the kitchen. That was my first impression of her, her laugh. You can tell a lot, I think, from a person's laugh, and hers was too loud, what my mother would have described as "brawling," and it went on for too long. I paused inside the passage a moment, getting beyond the stereotype that laughter presented in my mind, then closed the front door loudly so they had an opportunity to compose themselves while I took off my coat before heading into the kitchen to meet her.

She was sitting on Ryan's lap when I entered the kitchen, jumped up when she saw me standing in the doorway, and quickly sat in the vacant seat beside his, laughing only slightly less loudly, with her hand covering her mouth in what seemed to me to be a display of false modesty, because obviously if she were genuinely modest, she would have gotten off his lap before I made my entrance so that it wouldn't be my first impression of her (discounting the one at the front door, which she might not have been aware had already been taken into account). Ryan looked slightly embarrassed, but also happy, and I got that. She was probably the first girl he liked who'd squirmed on his adolescent lap; of course he was ecstatic, but I was not.

When I'd pictured her in my mind throughout the day, I had imagined a girl who was really a female version of my son, demure and sensible, respectful and modest, bright and polite, convinced for some reason she would be a perfect balance of prettiness, braces, and glasses. This girl was the antithesis of my vision. She was *street*, that was the word that came to my mind, *pure street*, one of those kids who are always outside their yard from the time they learn to unlock the front door and let themselves out. She was a blurred amalgamation of huge hooped earrings, permed, gelled hair, and short skirt with three-quarter-length socks that ended above her knees and below her skirt, like stockings lacking only the garter. She had managed to make her school uniform look like party attire with her cuffs and sleeves rolled up till they ended above her elbows, and a bold collection of clackety bangles adorned her wrists. Too many undone top buttons at the front of her shirt had resulted in an ample display of cleavage. She *was* pretty, that part I had been right about, but it was a kind of vulgar beauty. She was small, a lot shorter than my gangling son, but fit, like a fully developed woman who'd squeezed herself into a girl's school uniform to make herself look sexy. Ryan looked at me and his face fell and I knew it was because of my expression, which I tried to soften, make it reflect something other than the thoughts going through my mind.

"Hello," I said.

In his attempt to greet me cheerfully I saw the effort he was making to mask the atmosphere I had created. He said, "Hi, Mum." Then he introduced the girl, but I misheard him. I thought he said, "This is my sweetie," and my response was angry. I said, "Your *what?*"

"Sweetie," she said, blowing a purple neon bubble in her gum till it popped, licking it back in, smiling. "Sweetie by name and sweetie by nature."

"That's a very unusual name," I said.

She told me the story of how she got her name like it was some huge jolly jape, and finished with "This is a lush house, man. I'd love to live here."

Yes, I thought, I bet you would.

While I was at work imagining the studious shy girl with

glasses and braces, I had thought I would give them space, respect their privacy in the communal parts of our home, but she scared me, the girl without a proper name, with the brawling laugh and jiggling D cups. Instead, I tidied up the kitchen around them and started preparing dinner, hardly wanted her to have a second alone with my virgin boy, because she wasn't the sort of girl my son would give a shy first kiss and fumble with for ten months, building up to his first experience of sex. She was the sort who might turn up to revision wearing no knickers! Grandmotherhood was sitting at my kitchen table blatantly taunting me and I'd be damned if my first grandchild was going to emerge from Sweetie's loins.

She stayed about an hour after I arrived back home, and after she left, Ryan went upstairs to his room without speaking to me. He was disappointed in me. He didn't say it out loud, but I saw in his face that my attitude toward Sweetie had disappointed him. To be fair, it had disappointed me, but she had disappointed me, his choice had disappointed me. We were all put out, and frankly, I felt it was a small price to pay to have her gone from his life and a space left for the nice girl I knew was out there somewhere waiting. It wasn't the right time to have the fifty discussions with him I'd been planning all day, so I only said one thing, had to, sitting on the bottom of his bed speaking to the back he'd turned on me when I entered.

"Any girl you sleep with could end up being the mother of your child. Anything could happen; she forgot to take her pill, the condom broke, it was a risky time of the month, anything. If you have the urge to sleep with someone, remember that. And ask yourself if she's the kind of person you'd want to raise your kids."

Of everything I ever did as a parent, I regret that conversation the most. To be specific, I deeply regret the fact that it wasn't a conversation at all. I made a statement and simply expected him to follow through. We bought Sheba when Ryan was four and I spent hours discussing with him what we would name her, and the ways I thought his suggestion, Big Bird, could be improved on. I discussed such inconsequential things in such minuscule detail, and this one thing, so vast and new and so important to my son, this single issue I failed to discuss at all, just made my point then acted as if the matter had been concluded.

I know he spoke to her a couple of times after that on the phone, though I never heard the words he was saying, but I could tell from the tone of his voice and the defensiveness of his body language that it was her. The only other time I saw her was the day before Ryan died. She came in the evening and they talked briefly before I called him in. I wasn't exactly proud of myself, but I was glad it was a chapter we could close. Then after he died, was taken, I had expected to see her at the funeral amongst his friends, but she didn't show. It is probably a complete double standard, because I never mourned the fact of not seeing her till then, but since that day, my heart has held that particular absence against her.

Our legal team is already assembled in the court foyer when we arrive, with Kwame. I ask and Quigg tells me there is no word yet on whether Tyson Manley will give evidence. She outlines what to expect for the day, starting with St. Clare's cross-examination of Kwame and, depending how long it goes on for, the next witness, Nadine Forrester, the woman who actually saw Ryan's murder. Quigg apologizes to me in advance, says it will be hard to hear the details of her evidence, says I need to steel myself to sit through it, or to choose not to listen at all, to leave court till Nadine's evidence is done. I say I'll give it some thought, though I already know I will be in the gallery listening. Nipa has gone to get coffee for us both, and while I wait for her to return, I take a seat beside Kwame on the bench and Quigg reminds us not to discuss his evidence. I remember my dream. There are things I want to say to this man that make me feel deeply emotional. I have to avoid them, otherwise I will probably cry.

Instead I say, "You look tired."

"I couldn't really sleep properly."

"Valerian and vodka helps."

He smiles. "Maybe I'll give it a go. How're you bearing up?"

My eyes fill and I shrug. If I speak it will push me over the edge. One of the things I have discovered since the event is that I have the capacity to cry for hours. I struggle hard to get myself under control because I know that if I start I may not be able to stop. More than anything, I want to thank him for what he did for Ryan. One of the worst things for me has been imagining Ryan's last moments, imagining my son's blood oozing out onto the cold concrete ground, and Ryan afraid, in pain, alone, perhaps not knowing in that moment, not thinking about how much he was loved. Last night I dreamed again of his dying, but for the first time Kwame was with him, trying to save him, calling for help and doing everything he could so my son might live. Ryan still died in my dream, he always dies, over and over, night after night, I watch him die, but this time he was not alone. He was in this man's beautiful arms, strong and dark and vital as a baobab tree. I want to explain to him the comfort he has given me, and I will. I just can't do it now without falling apart. I take his hand in mine and squeeze it. He puts his other over mine and we sit like this in silence till Nipa returns.

Lorna arrives soon after. I finish my coffee and Nipa takes us up to the stairwell outside the public gallery. Luke and Ricardo are here again today, and I give them both a hug and thank them for coming. There are masses of people waiting, queuing down the stairwell for access to the public galleries of this and other courts. I try not to make it too obvious, but I scan the crowds looking for Ms. Manley, wondering if she will show up today and at what time. I cannot see her. She still has a son at home of school age, must surely be up to see he has something to eat and gets out of the house in good time to be punctual for school. But maybe she doesn't. Maybe her son gets himself up and ready, maybe she is fast asleep while he's rummaging for a clean shirt to wear, finding himself a bag of crisps or a couple of cookies to tide him over till lunchtime and free dinner. Perhaps lying in bed and sleeping is how she passes most of her day; that would make sense. It would explain what she was doing when her eldest son was being gunned down, while the other was sheathing his knife in preparation to leave her home. I look at my watch; it's almost ten. It would explain where she is right now.

Lorna leaves her bag with me and nips to the toilet in the few minutes left before they call us in. I place her bag on my lap and notice she has Friday's newspaper rolled up on top of it. I open it and begin skim reading the contents. On page five there are two photographs of Ryan and Tyson Manley side by side. The headline says "Trial Starts for 17 Year Old Accused of 16 Year Old's Fatal Stabbing." It states the case is being heard at the Old Bailey. It gives the date Ryan was killed, the place, mentions that Tyson Manley has recently turned seventeen but was sixteen at the time the stabbing occurred, that at the time of the murder, Ryan was carrying a knife. It says Ryan's death was the third London teenage stabbing fatality for the year and that this figure is a 25 percent decrease on available statistics for the same period last year. This decrease is a result of positive policing interventions and proactive campaigning in dealing with and raising the profile of youths caught up in gang culture.

Then I notice that neither photograph has a name below it and the omission devastates me, the idea that there may be people who saw this paper on Friday, not knowing whose picture was whose, thinking that Ryan, the gentlest of boys, could ever have willfully taken another person's life when he couldn't even harm a spider; took responsibility for catching them himself inside our home rather than take the chance of me or Lloydie killing them instead of taking the time to capture them without injury and put them outside. He would use a glass or cup with a sheet of paper beneath it and talk to them, explaining what he was doing while he carried them out, found somewhere to release them, then lowered the glass to ground level so they could wander off to freedom at their leisure.

We went to Center Parcs three Christmases ago, spent five days there, us three and Lorna and Leah. It snowed so much in the run-up, we were worried for days before that the weather would be too bad for us to drive there. We made it in the end, slowly, painstakingly. That year at Center Parcs was the closest we ever came to being in Lapland, so white everywhere, so much snow around us, and so much of it unbroken, or broken only by the footprints of birds, squirrels, deer.

We ventured out late on Christmas Eve dressed like skiers, bags on our backs packed with our swimming kits and towels, headed for the pool. As we walked along the path from our front door, Ryan noticed an earthworm just lying on top of the snow and ice. We wondered where it had come from, all plump and glistening as if it had just emerged from the earth below, which seemed impossible.

"Come on, guys," I said to Ryan and Leah, who were crouched on either side of it like it was the most fascinating thing they'd ever seen.

"We can't just leave her there," Ryan said. "She'll freeze."

"Worms aren't male or female, idiot," Leah said. "They're both."

"Don't call Ryan an idiot," Lorna said.

"Hermaphrodites," I said. "Worms are hermaphrodites. It'll be fine, come on, we're getting late."

"Hold on," said my son.

He pulled off his gloves and stuffed them into his pockets, carefully lifted up the worm, placed it onto his palm, then looked around. There was snow everywhere. Knowing he would not now abandon this creature, that our moving forward depended on first finding somewhere else for it to go, I looked around as well, wondering where the heck he could put it.

"Try the base of a tree," I said. The snow was beginning to thaw around the bases of the trees, not much and virtually imperceptible to anyone except individuals hell-bent on finding an earthworm a home.

He went to a tree—not even the one closest to him—picked up a piece of wood a little larger than a twig, and used it to loosen the earth around the base, scooped out the center of it, gently placed the worm in the crater he had created, and covered it with the soil he had just removed. He cleared his hands by vigorously wiping them against each other above the mound, determined not a particle would be wasted. When he finished, his expression was satisfied.

"Let's get out of here," he said, pulling his gloves back on.

All that trouble for a worm—that's what I was thinking as we carried on our way—*all that trouble for a bloody worm!* But if I had to bring everything he ever did in his life down to one act, highlight a single moment that defined my son, illuminated his heart, his soul, the very core of his being, it would be that moment at Center Parcs, on his way to have fun, taking the time to rescue a creature the majority of people would probably not even have noticed. The idea that anyone anywhere could look at my son's photograph and imagine for one second he was capable of killing another human being is enough to destroy me.

As I close the paper, roll it up, and put it back in the bag, Lorna returns and the security guard calls everyone waiting for Court 16 to take their seats in the gallery.

Tyson Manley is wearing another expensive suit today, in gray so shiny it is almost silver, with a black shirt underneath it, the top button undone, and a white tie draped around his neck, untied. I assume it's his mother providing the outfits he wears. If she were a close friend, I would advise her that instead of showing off his debonair wardrobe, she would do better to pick him up a somber, sensible suit from a cheap chain store, because today he looks like the human equivalent of a disco ball. It's only ten o'clock and he already looks bored.

St. Clare stands to cross-examine Kwame. He keeps his

hands benignly in the side trouser pockets of the tailored black suit he wears beneath his gown, and from where I am sitting I can see his shoes, black leather, expensive-looking, so highly polished they look patent. His accent is Eton and Oxbridge thoroughbred, his voice nasal and low, and the words drawl out of him in a manner that makes him sound tipsy. He wears what has to be the oldest wig in the court-room. It looks like it was white once, back in 1758 perhaps, and has been in the St. Clare family since, being passed from privileged eldest son to privileged eldest son through the centuries and generations to date, and it perches on his head like a filthy creature skinned by an insane taxidermist.

"Mr. Johnson, do you remember the statement you gave to the police on March 19?"

"Yes."

"The day after Mr. Williams was killed?"

"Yes."

"While the details were fresh in your mind?"

"Yes."

"You said you saw a person walking along the high street wearing a brown top embellished with a gold monogram, headed into the Sports Ground?"

"Yes."

"You stated, and I will quote directly from your statement here, 'I could not see his face. It was too dark.'"

Kwame does not respond.

"That is what you said, is it not?"

"Yes."

"Yet on Friday afternoon, standing in this court, some seven months after the event, you would have us believe you had excellent vision and lighting on the day in question, and no difficulty whatsoever identifying a person whom you glanced at for a second only, that you were able to recognize this person beyond any shadow of doubt?"

"Yes, I . . ."

"Well, which of these versions is the truth?"

A pause, then, "Both of them."

"*Both* of them?" St. Clare asks. He looks over at the jury and the emphasis he puts on the word *both* combined with that look seems to ask, "Can you believe a single word coming out of this man's mouth?"

"Yes. It was dark but . . ."

"Thank you, Mr. Johnson. I think we get the drift."

I look over at the faces of the jury, can see confusion has replaced the acceptance and empathy I saw on their faces on Friday.

"Can you confirm the trousers that person wore?"

"No."

"Or the color?"

"I don't know."

"You don't?"

"No."

"Can you confirm what he was wearing on his feet; boots, trainers, shoes?"

"No."

"A watch, any jewelry?"

"None that I saw."

"Are you saying the person was not wearing jewelry, or that you did not notice whether or not he was?"

"I didn't notice."

"I see. What about the woman who ran into you, who almost knocked you over, what about her? Can you recall what she was wearing?"

"Something white, or maybe gray . . ."

"Well, was it white or was it gray?"

"I'm not sure."

"Or some other color, even?"

"It was so fast . . ."

"Can you say with any certainty at all what she was wearing?"

A pause, then Kwame says, "No."

"What, not at all?"

"Not definitely."

"Yet you expect us to believe you when you say the person you saw in the brown top was Mr. Manley?"

"It was."

"So you have said. Mr. Johnson, would you agree that you are a particularly unreliable witness?"

Kwame is seriously ruffled. The annoyance in his voice is evident when he answers, "I don't agree with you, no."

"My Lord, I have no further questions for this witness," St. Clare says, closing the folder in front of him and sitting down. It is very subtle, that's what's clever about it, the subtlety. He hasn't actually said the words and he has not been melodramatic in his actions, yet I have the distinct impression St. Clare has stopped asking questions not because he's run out of them, but because it's pointless asking any more questions of someone so blatantly determined to lie. And some of the jurors are with him, not the older woman, the grandma, but three of the other women and two of the men, including the Indian guy. I can see on their faces that they are no longer sure whether Kwame is a reliable witness or not. I look at Tyson Manley, and for the first time, he seems to me to be engaged with his trial. It is faint but he is watching Kwame intently, and somewhere at the corners of his mouth is the beginning of a smile.

Quigg stands. "Mr. Johnson, may I please ask you a few more questions?"

"Yes."

"You've already told us of your work as a football coach?"

"Yes."

"Some of the boys you have worked with have gone on to be signed up by regional youth football clubs?"

"Yes."

"There must be a way of identifying which of these boys have the potential to be signed up, the ones who have the talent to make a professional career of footballing."

"There is."

"How do you tell?"

"I observe them, how they play, their coordination with the ball, their speed and agility."

"Is it fair to say you pay close attention to the bodies of your boys?"

"Excuse me?"

"I mean is it fair to say you pay close attention to how their bodies are used, how they move, walk, run?"

"Yes."

"When you identified Mr. Manley, was it because you saw his face?"

"No."

"Did you tell the police you had seen his face?"

"No, I did not."

"May I quote another extract to you from the statement you made on March 19?"

"Yes."

"You said, 'I knew it was Tyson Manley because I know how he carries himself, the way he moves.'"

"That's right."

"And that is the same as you told us in court on Friday?"

"It is."

"You have said you had a special interest in Mr. Manley?"

"Yes."

"Because of his family circumstances and the trouble he kept getting into."

"Yes."

"You wanted to help him?"

"Yes."

"And you hadn't had a falling-out; effectively, you parted on good terms?"

"Yes."

"Is there any reason why you would make up the fact that the person you saw on March 18 entering the Sports Ground was Tyson Manley?"

"No."

"If you had any doubt about the identity of the person you saw, any doubt whatsoever, would you have told the police the person you saw was Mr. Manley?"

"If I had any doubt, I wouldn't even have brung up his name."

Quigg repeats this slowly. "If you had any doubt, you would not even have brung up his name?"

"That's right."

"Thank you, Mr. Johnson. I have no further questions."

The judge excuses Kwame and he leaves the court. I am examining the jurors' faces, trying to tell what impact

Quigg's redress has had, but can't call it. The judge decides we should all have a twenty-minute break, and Lorna and I follow Nipa out.

We congregate in the stairwell and Nipa pops into the toilet while we're waiting.

"Bloody hell, Quigg did well to pull that back," Lorna whispers.

"Did you think it was enough?"

"Kwame was completely believable," Lorna says. "Even when that QC was calling him a barefaced liar. He's a deadly old man, looks like he's knocked back a bottle of whiskey on the way in, but he's got his wits about him, that's for sure."

"I can't believe he was so rude to Kwame."

"That's his job."

"What, treating people like shit?"

"He just wants to win and anywhere he can inject a bit of doubt into the minds of the jury, he will."

"Regardless of the truth?"

"Marcia, do you really think he gives a toss whether Manley's guilty or innocent? He just wants to win. This is all about scoring points, nothing more. And Quigg's no different. Do you think it's just coincidence that she happens to have a black male assistant working with her on this case? He's basically her antiracism proclamation, sitting there for the duration in case anyone doubts it. That'll gain her a couple of points in the minds of some of the jury at least."

If we were anywhere else, I would probably be shouting. In the stairwell, beneath the sign telling us not to discuss cases here, my words are a low and frantic hiss. "Oh my God! You're totally paranoid! You know, everyone everywhere isn't making some political point with everything they do. Why does poor Henry have to be some complicated plot for Quigg to prove she's not prejudiced? Why can't he just be the most qualified, capable person she could have chosen to bring along to help her?"

Nipa returns from the toilet and because of this the discussion comes to an abrupt end.

"So far so good," she says, and neither of us replies, though I give Nipa a small smile of acknowledgment.

"It's Nadine Forrester next, isn't it?" Lorna asks.

Nipa nods then says to me, "Her evidence is going to be pretty graphic, Marcia. Are you sure you want to be in there listening to it?"

"I have to, I don't have a choice."

"You do have a choice," Lorna says. "I'll be there. You don't have to."

"I want to know, . . ." I say. I don't explain it, the raw need for every detail, no matter how awful, how terrible, no matter what it contributes to my nightmares, my pain. I find it hard to understand myself. My son died horribly, in the most traumatic circumstances, and he did it without me. He didn't have the chance to opt out, and because he could not make that choice, I will not make it either. But it is so personal and I don't know if it is structurally sound, so I don't say it, can't take the risk of Lorna or Nipa taking this fragile logic apart. " . . . I *have* to know."

Lorna holds my hand, squeezes it, and says, "Okay."

Nadine Forrester is young and blond and nervous. Quigg does a good job easing her in gently, building a picture of a twenty-two-year-old who jogs four times a week, for differing durations, in different places, one of the regular places she jogged up until March 18 being the Sports Ground.

On March 18 at around six fifteen, she was on her second lap of the grounds, and Quigg guides the jury to the detailed map of the Sports Ground so they can see that she was in the final quarter of a clockwise circuit. There is a slight incline that meant she did not have a clear view of the entrance to the Sports Ground till she was about 800 meters away from it. This was the first point that she noticed Ryan ahead in the distance. She had her headphones in, was listening to garage music as she ran. She was vigilant, always is when she's running. She's had trouble with weirdos, been followed in the past, regularly had to deal with sexual innuendo and unwanted attention, so although she had her headphones in, she was fully aware of her surroundings and the people in her vicinity.

She is pretty, Nadine, maybe five seven or eight with a slim, athletic frame. I visualize her in running kit, with cropped pants and vest, her hair, which is down now, pulled into a ponytail behind her, and have no difficulty imagining men ogling and making comments as she passes.

Quigg asks, "Miss Forrester, what was Ryan doing when he first came into view?"

"He was too far away, I couldn't see what he was doing, but once he came into view I kept my eyes on him."

"At that point he was walking toward you?"

"Yes."

"But still some distance away?"

"Yes."

"Was there anyone else in the park?"

"No. I'd passed another guy who was jogging in the opposite direction a few minutes earlier, but no one else. That was one of the reasons I kept my eye on him. I thought about turning around and running the other way, to be honest, 'cause there weren't any other people near us and I didn't want my phone jacked . . ."

"As in stolen from you?"

"Yes."

"So you thought about turning around and going the other way."

"Yes."

"What stopped you?"

"As I got closer, I could see he was eating, looked like chicken and chips out of a box. That sort of made me feel a bit safer, not that you can't mug someone if you're eating, but it made me feel a bit safer, so I carried on."

She's blowing my mind. She sees my son walking in the park. He's not interested in her, not even glancing her way or paying her any attention. He's just in the Sports Ground, walking along, eating chicken and chips, wearing his football kit with his school blazer over it, and without knowing anything else about him, she's already associated him with phone-jacking and mugging.

Ryan slept over at Lorna's about a year ago. He got the bus to hers after school and stayed till the Saturday evening. He got home about sevenish, and when he entered the house, he slammed the front door. It was so uncharacteristic that I went straight out into the hallway to see what was wrong, and it was obvious he was upset, close to tears as he chucked his bag onto the floor, unzipped his body warmer.

"What's happened?" I asked.

"Nothing!"

"Tell me."

"What's the point? It doesn't change anything."

"Ryan, would you please talk to me? What's happened?"

"Nothing!" he said. "Nothing! I'm not exaggerating, *nothing* happened!"

"I don't understand."

"I got on the bus to come home. It was packed. I sat down. That's it. I wasn't doing nothing, just sat down and the old lady next to me moves over. There's nowhere to go, but she moves, scrunches herself up against the window—oh my days, if you saw her, all scrunched up, y'know—and she wraps *both* her hands around the handles of her bag like she's ready to fight me to stop me taking it. I never even noticed she *had* a bag. Up to then I never even really noticed her. Why's she gotta go on like that? Why?"

"She's an ignorant woman. You just have to ignore people like that . . ."

"I should ignore her? Why ain't *she* ignoring *me*? On my life, she made me so angry I wannid to take her stinking bag, not to rob her, I wannid to chuck it out the window, teach her a lesson. I came this close!" He put his thumb and index finger about a centimeter apart, demonstrating.

Obviously he didn't do it. Obviously I talked him down, appealed to the sensible, compassionate part of him that the stranger on the bus had snuffed out in a moment of ignorance. But it was on my mind for weeks after. He was fifteen. I was already steering him away from street kids toward friends of a higher caliber, I was preventing him from aimlessly hanging around by making sure his time was filled, nudging him toward study and books and everything that might ensure his future was bright, but I couldn't work out how to steer him clear of ordinary people in common spaces, had not brought him up like my mother had brought me up, telling me I needed to be twice as good as the next white person in order to get half as far. That woman on the bus, who probably didn't even think about him again once he'd got off at his stop, was in my head for weeks and I shared Ryan's anger. I know he would have been angry now listening to Nadine's racial profiling of him, while all he was doing was putting one foot in front of the other, going to pick up his stuff.

Quigg asks, "You were still jogging toward Ryan. You decided not to turn back. What happened next?"

"I was probably about a hundred meters away from him when I saw another guy behind him. He'd just entered the Sports Ground and he was walking quickly in the same direction as Ryan but was maybe two hundred meters away from him. I was close enough to Ryan to see his face. He had his headphones in his ears. I think he was listening to music, because he was walking like he was keeping time with the beat."

"Did he look at you?"

"No, he was looking at his food. I'm sure he must have noticed me but he wasn't actually leering."

"Can you describe the other person, the one who had just entered the Sports Ground?"

"It was dark and he was wearing a hoodie. I couldn't see his face. I thought about turning around again, but I felt safer because I was almost level with Ryan, so I wasn't the only person about."

"And what happened next?"

"I passed Ryan. He didn't look at me. But the other guy, I was running toward him but I still couldn't see his face even though I was only about a hundred and fifty meters away, and that was freaking me out a bit. Anyway, I carried on jogging toward him. He was walking really fast toward me and he seemed to be getting faster and then it was like he was running toward me and I nearly freaked out completely. I thought he was gonna attack me. After I started running, 'cause of a couple of incidents, I started going to tae kwon do, and when he was running toward me, I was thinking about stance, the best way to use his own force against him or block him if he went for me; it's like my mind had slowed down and I was trying to be prepared for attack, and then he ran past me . . ."

"I want to stop you there for a moment. Can you describe that person?"

"It was all so fast and I couldn't see his face 'cause his head was down, like he was looking at the ground."

"What about his clothing? Did you notice what he was wearing?"

"Black jogging bottoms and trainers; Nike Flynit Maxes. He had on a top, kinda dark brown, and it had a logo on it, a yellow one, and his hood was up. The hood was black."

"Did you notice anything in particular about the way he walked?"

"He was running."

"Before he started running. Did you notice anything unique or characteristic about the way he walked?"

"No."

"What about his height?"

"He was taller than me, a lot taller, about six foot, maybe six two."

Her estimation of the person's height is spot on; Tyson Manley is six foot one.

"Could you see if he was carrying anything?"

"Not in his left hand. He passed me on the left. That hand was empty. But even when he was coming toward me I couldn't see his right hand because he kinda kept it behind his back. I was thinking he had a knife, then I was thinking I was overthinking and he probably didn't have anything in his hand, and I was telling myself to stay calm, 'cause if I panicked I wouldn't be able to defend myself. As he passed me he really started sprinting and I was relieved he had passed me but I looked back to make sure, in case he came at me from behind."

"When you looked back, what did you see?"

"He stabbed him. In the back. I couldn't believe it. I tripped and fell over. He just ran up behind Ryan and stabbed him! It was horrible, horrible!" Her composure has disintegrated. She is crying and it is easy to imagine that she is experiencing in the detailed recall the same level of incomprehension and shock she experienced at the time it happened. "He pulled the knife out and he stabbed him again. Ryan hadn't even turned around. The first stab was like a punch and it kinda pushed Ryan forward a bit and then he stabbed him again and this time Ryan started turning around and he pulled the knife out and stabbed him again, and then Ryan fell. He just fell onto the ground, onto his knees then his stomach, and the hoodie still stabbed him again in the back. He went down on one knee so he was half kneeling beside him and he stabbed him again, the fourth stab, while he was lying on the ground. And then he looked up and saw me, and I've never ever in my life ever been that scared because I was a witness, I'd seen it all, and I thought he was going to come and stab me as well and I just got up and ran for my life. I thought he was chasing me and I ran. And when I got to the entrance there was another black guy there and I think I just screamed. Then he ran into the grounds and I ran across the road into the Turkish supermarket. I had scraped both my knees and my hands, and they were bleeding but I never even noticed till I got in there and they were ringing the police, that's how scared I was. It's the worst thing I've ever seen. I can't even walk past the grounds now, even now I can't."

I am crying silently and Lorna is too. This is how he was taken, my son, so mercilessly. Tyson Manley didn't walk up to him and face him like a man and tell him what the problem was, so that if there was any possibility of it being sorted out, it could be. He never gave him a chance to explain or defend himself. How Nadine has described it is exactly how I have relived it, imagining Ryan walking along listening to his music and eating his hot wings and chips, because he loved hot wings. He would have been tired after training and he was just chilling, walking back to get his boots, just chilling with his food and his music, so unprepared that when it happened, instead of thinking about how much he was loved, instead he was wondering *Why?* Why was he being attacked, stabbed, why was he dying? *Why?* What for?

Tyson Manley is looking down at the floor. He makes no eye contact with anyone in the court. There is a scuffling sound from behind me and I turn my head to see Luke standing, with tears on his face, pointing at Tyson Manley and shouting, "Murderer! Murderer!" Then there are other voices, Ricardo's trying to calm him down, Nipa's as she rises, the security guard's as the door is flung open and she enters. The judge directs the public gallery to be cleared and says we will have a half-hour recess. The jury begins to leave and Tyson Manley is taken out, and Lorna and Nipa have to help me to stand so we can leave the gallery, because my legs are unsteady, their strength fails me.

At the top of the stairwell I hug Luke to comfort him, feel his distress in the tension of his body, so tall and so strong, yet he is just a child, like Ryan was. His are the words I wish I had shouted myself. I understand his outrage, his need to rail against the wickedness of his best friend's life so coldly taken. For what? That's what I need Sweetie to tell me. Why. Lorna suggests Luke gets some air, goes with him and Ricardo down the stairs and outside. The other people who have also been expelled from the public gallery try to not make it obvious they are watching and listening, like people pretending to have stopped watching the TV just as the exciting film they've been watching reaches its climax.

I go to the toilet with Nipa, wash my face, blow my nose, attempt to compose myself. We stay in there a long while and she talks to me though I can hardly focus on her words, about strength and justice for Ryan. She speaks of justice as if it is the same as reparation, but it's not. Lloydie's right. This trial, all this evidence, these details I am sitting through, what's the point of it? What has been done is too unjust to ever be put right. What difference does being here make?

Lorna and the boys return soon after we emerge from the toilets and we wait in silence for security to say we can go back in. Tyson Manley is expressionless while the judge gives the gallery a severe telling off. We are warned that being in the public gallery is a privilege, not a right, and that if there are any more outbursts he will have the gallery cleared.

The jury is brought back in and Quigg continues, and it is even worse. She wants specifics. The jury has to know how Tyson Manley ran, whether Nadine is sure there wasn't anything characteristic about the way he moved (she didn't notice). She wants Nadine to demonstrate how the right arm was being held as Tyson Manley ran toward her, the very angle so the jury can see how a cold-blooded murderer carries their weapon into the kill. She has Nadine demonstrate the actual stabs. The first one is like a fierce bowler throwing the cricket ball overarm toward the batsman and wicket, full swing. She wants to know about the knife, the very length of the blade; about twenty centimeters, like the knife Nadine's father uses on Christmas day to slice the family's turkey. She has to know how Tyson Manley came down to his knee; hard, he fell onto his knee hard with all his body weight. Which knee? The right one. Hard enough to leave a bruise or graze or cut? Yes, Nadine wouldn't be surprised if it had. And any reaction, any gesture, any word from my son while this terrible assault was being meted out, any response or sound from him at all? None, he was completely taken by surprise, he didn't have a chance.

I cry all the way through this part of her evidence. I try to keep it as quiet as I can so that my feelings do not interfere with the machinations of the court, so my grief does not hamper this legal process—or get us thrown out. Throughout, I watch Tyson Manley. I want to see some sign from him, some indication he understands the magnitude of what he has done. I want to see guilt, discomfort, the smallest gesture of remorse, but his expression is unchanged. As distraught as I am, I realize I made an error before in my assessment of him; I thought he was arrogant, filled with machismo, cold, but I was wrong; he is simply indifferent. Nothing moves or touches him because there is nothing in him to be moved or touched. I don't know where such a vacancy comes from, how it is possible for a human being to have as little feeling as a puppet or paper doll. What difference will it make if he is found guilty and punished, sent to prison, given life? He is as indifferent as the judge's bench, the glass cage he sits inside, the metal blade of the knife he used on my boy.

So far there's been no sign of Ms. Manley. I'm sure, like me, she knew what evidence we were going to be hearing today. I would love to think that shame has kept her away, that she was worried she might not be able to successfully carry out her posing and posturing on the end of the bench while I sat hardly more than a meter away from her stylish handbag, weeping, but somehow I doubt it. The values—or lack of values—her son has, he's learned at home, from babyhood, as a toddler, a boy too young for nursery school; he's learned from her. I would love to think she isn't here because she's embarrassed by the notion that her son's actions reflect on her as a mother. But if I was forced to put my money where my mouth is, I'd bet she simply couldn't be arsed to get out of bed.

Quigg's questions go on till almost one, when the court breaks for everyone to have lunch. I leave a different woman to the one I was this morning. It feels like what little was left of my heart has been smashed to smithereens.

5

WE GO TO LUNCH WITH Luke and Ricardo, to a sandwich shop nearby, where the boys have soup and sandwiches and crisps, knock it back like they could order and finish the same amount again, which is how Ryan ate; I had forgotten that, born hungry and it never changed. When people asked me how he was, I used to joke that he was very well but eating us out of house and home. Those wings and chips he ate on March 18 wouldn't have been his dinner. He was just snacking after football and would still have had room for dinner if he'd made it home. It worries me constantly that I will start forgetting him, forget over time the way he was. I'm glad they came with us to lunch. It's such a small detail but I need every memory of him I can gather. I'm so grateful they helped me remember the way my son ate.

"I don't know what St. Clare's gonna ask in his cross-exam," Lorna says. "There's nothing in Nadine's testimony that really affects his defense. It's not like she actually recognized Manley. She just saw a guy in a hoodie. Maybe it wasn't necessary to have all those details. It was horrible to hear and I don't really see that it contributed to the case against him."

"Sorry," Luke says, "I never meant to say nothing. I just kinda lost it."

"We all lost it a bit," Lorna says. "I just hope all that detail is over now."

I think of Lloydie saying, "Over? It's already over." All that happened this morning is that my waking imagination and dreams now have yet more violent detail to flesh them out. Those images in my mind that I'm constantly trying to steer clear of, avoid, that surprise me in my day-to-day life, the vivid flashbacks that appear unbidden in the middle of the most mundane tasks, will they ever be over? If so, when?

"Do either of you actually know Tyson?" Nipa asks. "Did you know him before?"

Before, a different era, the Before and the After, lifelines severed by a distinct demarcation forever. The life I lead now is in the After. The boys both shake their heads. Ricardo says, "He's not from our manor. He never went to our school. I heard of Vito, his brother, heard about the shooting and that, but I didn't know him."

"What about Sweetie?" Lorna asks.

Luke says, "Everyone knew her. All the boys, anyway. 'Cause she was older than us, we kinda looked up to her. She had a bit of a mouth on her though. Couldn't really tell Ryan what to do, but she wasn't his type."

Ricardo says, "Opposites attract, bro."

Opposites is right. Her world and my son's were light-years apart.

"Is she still at school?" I ask.

They both shake their heads. Luke says, "Ain't really seen her since then. Tell a lie, I seen her once, that's it."

"Did you talk to her about what happened?" Lorna asked.

They shake their heads. Ricardo says, "She never spoke to no one. Maybe she just came in to get her stuff, 'cause she was with the head of the sixth form and I never saw her at school after that."

We finish up and walk slowly back. The journalists are camped on the other side of the street from the main entrance. They watch us and snap a few photographs as we pass.

Lorna glares at them, her expression full of contempt. Under her breath she hisses, "Parasites!" as we turn into the alleyway leading to the entrance to the galleries. We climb the stairs to the second floor, then stand around and wait.

St. Clare's cross-examination is a short one. He wants to know if Nadine is able to identify the person who murdered Ryan, and she isn't. Can she categorically even say the person she saw was definitely a black man? First of all she says yes, but following a discussion of the lighting, the shadows, the brevity of her glance at his face, her fear, she allows that it was a man, but he could have been Indian, mixed race, Hawaiian, tanned. He wants to know how specific her estimation of the person's height was. The murderer could have been a couple of inches shorter or taller than she estimated. She concedes that because she was so afraid and because she herself was smaller, she may have seen the danger, the person, as bigger than they actually were. He has her confirm that on March 19 she took part in an identity parade at the police station in which the defendant was present and that she did not identify him as the man she saw in the park who had carried out the murder. St. Clare successfully makes the point that it could have been absolutely anyone who killed my son that day, and while her evidence gives us a clear picture of what happened to Ryan, there is no link between that evidence and Tyson Manley whatsoever.

We are talked through a short piece of CCTV footage by a police officer. It was taken from a security camera on the forecourt of a petrol station, and on it we see the murderer from the back as he passes the camera. The images are slightly grainy, but it is clear he is wearing a brown top, the hood up, black sweatpants, and trainers. From his gait, he seems young, fairly tall. He walks fast and has a pronounced bounce to his step, like the exaggerated bounce described by Kwame during his evidence. His hands must be in his front pockets, because you do not see them at all in the short clip, but even without really seeing anything of the person, even if I knew nothing of this case and was looking at the clip in isolation and unconnected with this trial, I would have guessed from the way he walks that he is a young black man.

The most useful thing about the clip is the time and date that pulse in the bottom left corner of the screen, March 18 at 18:32. This is consistent, Quigg says, with a fast walk from the Sports Ground directly after the murder if the murderer's destination was Sweetie Nelson's home. She directs the jury to another and less detailed map, which shows the Sports Ground marked "1" where Ryan was killed and Sweetie's home, marked "3." The most direct route between these two points is highlighted in yellow, and almost midway along that yellow route is "2," the spot at which the CCTV image was filmed.

Then Quigg reads out a statement from the arresting officer, dated March 19, the summary of which is that following the report of the murder and acting on pertinent information received, a warrant was issued for Tyson Manley's arrest and the officer was dispatched to the home of the suspect's mother, his place of abode, on the evening of March 18. Despite her saying her son was not there, the premises were searched, and on not finding him, a decision was made to set up surveillance on the premises so that if the suspect returned he could be apprehended.

Tyson Manley arrived back at the parental home the following morning at 09:00 on foot, and was first cautioned and subsequently arrested. He struggled with the arresting officers and was forcibly restrained. The handcuffs were applied, checked for tightness, and double-locked. A van was called and the suspect was conveyed to the police station, wherein he was booked by the custody sergeant and body mapping was requested.

Quigg reads the jury the caution text, confirms this had been read to Mr. Manley at the time of the arrest, advising him of his rights. I can only imagine the purpose of this is to ensure that further down the line, when looking at grounds for appeal, no one can say the boy who had so newly murdered my son had been deprived of any of his rights. It is almost four thirty by the time she is finished, and the case is adjourned till tomorrow morning at ten.

As we exit the court building, cameras begin to flash from the journalists on the pavement on the other side of the street. Nipa has her arm through mine and begins to steer me in the direction of the car park when Lorna says, "Hold on, I've got a statement I'd like to make." We have not discussed this, she and I, so I am caught on the hop and I run my hands over my face to ensure it is tear-free and pat my wig to confirm it is sitting where it should be. Nipa enlists the help of two officers standing nearby and, informing the media that a statement is to be made, the cameras are permitted to come closer, to form an arc around us and dangle huge microphones above our heads. Luke and Ricardo stand with us, their expressions serious. Lorna takes out Friday's paper, opens then folds it at page five, and points to the image of Ryan.

She says, "This is my nephew, Ryan Williams. He was the only nephew I had. He called me 'Teelor.' When he was a baby learning to talk, he couldn't say 'Auntie Lorna,' it was too much of a mouthful, he could only manage 'Teelor,' and it was so cute and lovely we kept it. It's what he always called me, right up to the end. I cannot begin to explain to you how special he was, or how much we loved him, or how devastated his murder has left us as a family." She points to the other image. "This is Tyson Manley. He is being tried for my nephew's murder. The next time you print something about this case, have the fucking decency to put their names to their photographs. They're two black boys, but they're not interchangeable. Thank you."

There are flowers, a couple of bouquets of daisies, and a teddy bear outside the garden on the pavement when I arrive back at my home with Nipa.

"Would you like me to move them?" Nipa asks. "Shall I take them inside for you?"

"It's fine," I say, as I get out of the car. "Leave them there." We say goodbye, and she leaves. There is a small card pinned to the teddy bear. The message on it reads "2 many stars in heaven already, Y did they have 2 take U? RIP. Ayeesha. X."

My eyes fill. It is my perpetual state, the tears so constantly near, the battle to contain them great because the one to make them stop is even greater. In the weeks after the event, this strip of pavement became a kind of memorial to Ryan, a shrine. There were masses of flowers and teddies and cards, candles and crucifixes, and in one case, three packets of Skittles from someone who obviously knew they were his favorite sweets. People I knew and total strangers visited and left small tokens then. Perhaps some of them have read about the trial and taken the time and trouble to remind me they exist and still care. It is astonishing, the beauty in humanity that sometimes accompanies the most hideous tragedy. They move me now as deeply as they did then. I don't pick them up, I leave them where they are, a proclamation to the world that something heinous has occurred, wondering for the millionth time whether my son can see them, whether despite the fact he may not have been thinking about it in his final moments, he has come to know since how much people care, how much we care, longing from the depths of my heart to believe it so.

Lloydie is not inside our home when I enter, but he has cooked dinner again and the pots are still warm and sitting on the stove. I pour myself a vodka, notice it is becoming my first act now when I arrive home, irrespective of the time. I have the drink but cannot eat. My stomach is unsettled and, at the same time, tight. I phone my mother before she phones me, settle on my bed, and tell her about the court day. Afterward I lie on top of the bedclothes, thinking I might have a quick nap because I feel so exhausted, but it doesn't come. I lie wide awake till quarter to six, then go to the bathroom and freshen up.

Hulya's is a gentrified deli-café with six or seven small

tables, two of which are occupied when I enter, and as I sit there waiting for Sweetie to arrive, there is a steady flow of takeout customers who come in to buy hot drinks and rolls and sandwiches, pay, and go. I am early by about ten minutes, so I order a coffee and settle at a table near the back where the seats are side on and I have a clear view of everything inside the small building, including Sweetie if and when she finally gets around to showing up. All the while I am berating myself for being here at all, watching both the café entrance and the clock.

It is ten to seven by the time she arrives, my coffee long finished. Close up I can see she has put on a little weight since I last saw her, much of it in her breasts, which are fuller than they were a year ago. She sports an afro, a large one, kinky-messy, as if she put her hair in twists last night and today has simply taken the twists out. I think it suits her. Its size makes her face look smaller and because of that, her eyes and mouth are larger focal points. But I can also see life has not been kind to her. What made her look "street" before was her attire and accoutrements. Now there is hardness in her gaunt cheeks, around the shadows beneath her eyes, about the ridge of her nose, which looks like it has been broken at some point and reset, in the quickness of the movement of her eyes. They dart around constantly, warily, checking out every movement and sound. The skin on her face and her hands is dry. She sits in the chair opposite me and we both look at each other in silence till she finally looks away.

I am clear this is not a cozy coffee meeting to catch up with a friend and I'm determined I will not make small talk. "Well?" I say.

"I didn't think you'd come."

"Well, I have, as you see."

The waitress comes over, takes her order for a hot choco-late and mine for another coffee, then goes away.

"How's the case going? D'you think Tyson's going down?"

"Is that why you asked me here? To find out about the case?"

"Yeah . . . no, not really."

"I haven't got time for games, Sweetie," I say, annoyed with the girl before me, but even more annoyed with myself and the hope that has dragged and kept me seated here, my pathetic pursuit of the truth, which made it impossible not to come, even though, as Lloydie would have asked, "What dif-ference does it make?" My annoyance cushions itself in anger. I pick up my handbag, about to stand.

"Wait. Don't go. I have to tell you something."

"What are you going to tell me? That your friend killed my son? That you lied to the police when you said he was with you that day? I don't need the courts to tell me what I already know. What I don't know is why. That's why I'm here, no other reason."

She is crying. The only sign of it is the tears rolling from her eyes. She doesn't hold her head in her hands like Lloydie, or howl aloud like I have. Her crying doesn't even impact on her features, the tears just run and she wipes them away with her fingertips. She was a year older than Ryan, seventeen now, nearly eighteen, still a child herself really, in legal terms.

"You set him up, didn't you? What do they call them? Honey traps? Is that what you were, some kind of honey-trap girl?"

She shakes her head. "I would never've done that. I know you don't believe me, but I swear to God, cross my heart and hope to die, I loved Ry. I loved him."

"You didn't even come to his funeral."

"I wannid to come, you don't know how bad I wannid to."

"But?"

She looks at me a moment, then away. "I never had nothing to wear."

I can't bring myself to respond to that. What would be the point? She needed to look good, to pose even there, and had nothing new or expensive enough to do that in. I will not sink to her level, will not have a discussion about the fact she could have turned up in anything, or point out it wasn't actually a rave we hosted that day; the people who showed up were there to support us, to bury my son.

I say, "I want to know what happened."

"He left a message. On my phone. Tyson heard it. I told Ryan not to call me. I told him to leave me alone, but he never listened. I warned him, but he was different . . . like there was too much trust in him. He never even wannid the knife . . ."

"You gave him a knife?"

She nods, because that's the kind of gift people like her give to those they love, not aftershave or champagne or forget-me-nots, they give metal gifts, murder weapons. If Tyson Manley had walked up to Ryan and faced him like a man, if he'd given my son the smallest fighting chance, Ryan could have whipped out her gift and used it to defend himself, maybe killed Tyson Manley accidentally instead of being killed himself, and I could have been sitting in court this week exactly where I've been sitting, except instead of staring at Tyson Manley wondering how he could have done it, I'd be looking down at Ryan gazing out from behind the glass. This is the thinking of people whose lives end too early and badly. I shake my head.

"And now you're gonna lie, go into court and tell them you were with Tyson when it happened so he can get away with it and next time you find some other patsy, you can give them another knife and he can kill them as well?"

"You don't know what it's like . . ."

"I know about the ridiculous code you all live by, the wall of silence, no one grassing, no one coming forward to tell the police the truth. It doesn't make things better. It's not noble. It's not cool. All it does is let people who've done wrong get away with it."

"Cool? You think I'm tryin'a play it cool? I go in there and say what you want me to say, you think that suddenly everything's gonna flip right? That I get to carry on like nothing went down?"

"If you tell the truth he'll go to prison. That's the reality. That's where this will end."

"If I tell the truth this'll never end, never! Man, you don't know the people I'm dealing with. You don't know my life. There is no *end*. Ain't no cavalry on the way, you get me? Ain't no one out there rescuing people like me! If I weren't dead by the time they finished, I'd wish I was."

All those things I did for Ryan, putting the safety locks on the kitchen drawers so he couldn't get at the sharp utensils that could harm him, the safety wheels on the back of his bike so he wouldn't fall off, and the helmet, so if he did he wouldn't crack his skull and die, walking him to school every morning till he was ten so no one could abduct him, because if he wasn't abducted, he couldn't be hurt; all those precautions and she slipped in anyway, bringing with her the boogeyman of my nightmares that I told my son did not exist.

"So you're really gonna do it, stand there and lie?"

"I have to."

"No. You choose to."

"Listen, I don't choose! I do what I gotta do."

I look at her, shake my head in disgust. "And this love you say you have for Ryan, that's how you show it? Telling lies to protect his killer."

"They know where to find me. I got no place else to go. You got no clue the things they'd do, the things they've already done . . ."

She looks up as the bell above the door chimes and two young women enter the café, about her age, with that look about them that I associate with Sweetie. I see on her face an expression of total fear and simultaneously she stands, lifting her side of the table with both hands as she does so, and everything on top of it, my coffee, her hot chocolate, the salt and pepper and condiments and menu fly off the table onto me and I tumble backward off my chair onto the floor, where I am too surprised to do anything other than look up at her in shock as she screams, "I'm warning you, you better stay the fuck away from me!"

Then she passes them as she walks out, and they watch her do so, before giving me a long hard stare, turning around, and leaving as well, without having purchased anything. The waitress, as stunned as I am, runs over, helps me up. Two other customers right the table and chairs and pick up the other items spilled across the floor. The manager asks if I am okay as I pull my purse out of my bag and struggle with fingers shaking so badly I am unable to pick out the coins. I give up, pull out a note instead, hand it to him, answer, "Yes."

When he gives me my change, I take it then find myself hesitating. Instead of leaving, I look out of the window, checking the street to make sure I can't see them anywhere, that those girls have actually gone, before opening the door and venturing out. I walk away from Hulya's on legs that are little more than jelly.

I catch a cab to Lorna's house, bang on her door.

"What's happened?"

I tell her pretty much word for word everything Sweetie said. I read from notes hastily scribbled on scraps of paper from my handbag while sitting in the backseat of the cab on the way over, trying to write it all down while it was still fresh in my mind.

"We've gotta ring Quigg and tell her," I say. "Even if Sweetie refuses to tell the truth, I will. I'll tell the jury what she told me. No one's gonna believe her word against mine."

"Are you mad?" Lorna asks. "You think you can just tell Quigg you've been meeting with witnesses, discussing the trial? They'll throw the bloody case out! And if by some miracle they didn't, why would they believe you? You're Ryan's mum. That defense QC would have a field day. He'd make mincemeat out of your impartiality. No, you can't tell anyone."

"So what, just let him get off? Keep my mouth shut as well and let that murderer walk? There is no evidence against him, not a single piece of evidence that links him directly to the murder, you know that."

"That boy's got no chance! Not only are they gonna convict him, he's gonna get a longer sentence than he would've if he wasn't black. The conviction stats don't lie."

I look at my sister in astonishment. "Are you totally insane? I want him convicted because he's guilty! I want him to be given the longest sentence they can give him because he's sucked the air from my life! What I want is justice, not racism, justice!"

"Marcia, he did it! We know he did. Every piece of circumstantial evidence leads to that conclusion. He's not going to get away with it."

"So your advice is to do nothing, say nothing? I don't know if I can."

"I'm telling you you can and you must," my sister says. Worse, I know she's right. I have to suck it up. Another thing to swallow and keep down, just one more thing to be silent about when I'm already so full I could burst.

Lloydie is at home when I get back. He is sitting at the kitchen table with Pastor Meade, who is speaking to him about strength. Erin and Paloma are also there, my line manager and colleague, friends from my years at the call center, just passing through, they say, and stopped off to see how I was getting on. They have brought us flowers, a beautiful bouquet that must have cost a fortune, and a huge card from the people I work with, filled with messages of support, reminding me that everyone is thinking of me, that Lloydie and I are in their prayers. I try to keep up a front, the practiced front of married couples to the world, hiding the separateness that has grown between me and Lloydie, presenting the unity it has become my sole responsibility to exhibit, but it has never been harder to do than it is at this moment. My emotions have been on the roller-coaster ride of their life. I tell them a bit, some of the details of the trial. My heart isn't in it, but I tell them anyway, because they're here and I can't get out of it, and while I do, from time to time, I gaze at Lloydie to see if he's listening and he doesn't look like he is. He gives the impression of being so engrossed in what the pastor is saying to him that he cannot focus on the latest developments of the police and the judicial system and their efforts to bring the murderer of our son to account.

I listen to myself from a distance, hear the sound of my own voice, my words, wonder how I am managing to speak to them, to carry on. Erin and Paloma, Pastor Meade, they just want to help us somehow, to do something, anything, but civility feels like a Herculean task, one that this evening is almost beyond me.

Finally I just have to tell them I'm truly exhausted and my head is pounding, that I need to have a bath and lie down. After the women go, I leave Lloydie and Pastor Meade to talk alone, and take valerian and vodka and paracetamol then get into the tub. I hear the front door open and close while I am in there and I wonder if Lloydie has gone out, but when I come out of the bathroom he is sitting on the bed with his face in his hands. He looks up at me. I am doing all I can to hold it together. On the outside, I am looking after myself, wearing my wig, plastering over the gaps and defects, creating a facade for the world that cloaks the anguish inside me, the circuits that no longer work, the bits that are broken, the pain.

Lloydie looks like I feel. It's all there; the anguish in his eyes, despair in the slump of his posture, anxiety in the prominence of the veins that crisscross his bony arms and hands, and it makes me angry, his collapse, because it sucks from me the right to have any expectation of him, makes me feel cruel for expecting more when he looks so pathetic, is being so pathetic. I go around to my side of the bed, sit on the edge of it to cream myself so I do not have to look at him and feel guilty, so I don't have to try to find surplus strength to compensate for his, when I can barely find my own.

He says, "I don't know how to do this. I just don't know."

As if there is a book, an instructional DVD that tells people how and what to do when their son is murdered, a manual that takes them through the process chapter by chapter, step by step.

"I had a plan. It wasn't big. It was a small one, but it was mine."

I say, "It's been seven months, Lloyd. You can't just keep going round it . . ."

"I reminded him . . ."

"I can't do this again."

"It's all I think about . . ."

"This isn't your fault."

He says, "You should never have married me."

And I ping from anger to open fury. I can't do it, can't do it for us both. I can't repair myself, and he's asking me to repair him. As though it comes from outside. As though self-repair is a wall hanging you can simply take down and wrap around yourself. As though you can do nothing, just wallow and surrender and somehow it can all be made good. His is the wish of a child; if I'd never married him, we would never have had Ryan, and he would never have had this hurt. But this pain is the evidence Ryan existed, was here, that for sixteen years he filled our home, our lives, with joy. I do not want this pain either, but if I were forced to choose, forced to make a choice between having my son followed by this pain or not having him at all, I would choose Ryan, always Ryan, every time.

"Well, I *am* your wife. And you're a man. Try acting like one!"

I know as soon as those words leave my mouth how cruel they are. I regret them even before my mouth closes, know I should take them back, apologize, that I have hurt him terribly when he is already finding it impossible to cope. I feel his movement within the mattress beneath me, know he is standing on the other side of the bed. He doesn't take a step, just stands there. Maybe he has things lined up to say, is trying to put them into an order or arrangement of some kind. Maybe he is trying to think of a response. Perhaps my words have cut him so deeply he can think of no response, because in the end he doesn't say anything, just gently pulls the bedroom door in behind him as he leaves.

Instead of running after him, I put on my nightie. Instead of apologizing, I get between the sheet and the duvet. Instead of saving my marriage, I turn off the bedside light. Then, having condemned him in my mind for wallowing and doing nothing, I lie alone in the darkness and cry.

The next morning when I wake, there is no cup of tea on the side and Sheba is curled up at the bottom of the bed.

Kwame has come along today, sits in the gallery behind us, beside Luke and Ricardo, whom he knows. I am really happy to have him here, hope somehow Ryan knows, can see, the Ryan who belonged to me and not to Sweetie. Last night in my dreams, he kissed me goodbye at the kitchen table, and as he turned to leave, I heard the sound of a small heavy object as it hit the laminated floor, looked down to see he'd dropped a knife. When I looked back up at his eyes, he had closed them. I need to reconcile the son I loved so carefully with the one who carried the gift from the girl without a proper name.

The court session starts with a legal argument over the body-mapping images before the jury is called in. The body maps show a number of injuries to Tyson Manley's body when he was arrested, but St. Clare points out that the police used an amount of force when they arrested Mr. Manley and that some of the injuries can be referenced to the arrest. His concern is that the jury might erroneously conclude that the injuries were attributable to the incident with the deceased when in fact they were not. He makes it clear there is no suggestion the police had beaten the defendant in some improper manner, but it was a violent arrest and injuries were sustained. Quigg agrees it would be an artificial exercise to try to marry up each injury, but these were the injuries on the body of the defendant at the time of the arrest and they can be presented to the jury with an explanation of the circumstances of the arrest so that the evidence is not misleading.

The judge ponders this, seemingly swayed by both arguments. Then, as if thinking aloud, he suggests to St. Clare that the jury may be able to reach their own conclusions if the evidence is correctly presented. St. Clare overplays his hand, snaps, rather peevishly, I think, that His Lordship's mind works very quickly, perhaps quicker than some of the jury members. From the judge's expression, it is clear he has taken as much affront at having his jury called stupid as he would have if St. Clare had thus insulted his kin. The judge decides the jury can be shown the body-mapping images and have the custody nurse talk them through. The jury is brought back in and the custody nurse practitioner is called to give her evidence.

As she gets into the witness box, Ms. Manley arrives alone, wearing her oversized dark glasses, dolled and made up in designer gear, reeking of perfume, carrying a different expensive handbag from the one she sported on Friday. Tyson Manley notices her, gives her a slight nod of the head in acknowledgment, then returns to watching the case unfold. It is almost eleven and I am disgusted with this woman who managed yesterday not to show up at all and who today has shown up late.

The custody nurse practitioner takes the stand in full nursing uniform, as though she has worn it specifically to quell the doubts of anyone who suspects she may be lying about the work she does for a living. Quigg explains to the jury that the purpose of this witness is to catalogue the injuries on the defendant's person at the time of the arrest, but not to ascribe to each injury a cause. She takes the nurse through the essentials, her name, that she has been employed by the Metropolitan Police Service for twenty-six years, that her role is to examine, treat, advise, and take samples from people who have entered police custody. She was on duty on March 19 and was asked by the custody sergeant on that date to body-map any visible injuries on the defendant's person, including those caused by the police during arrest. Again, in case of suspicion that any of Tyson Manley's human rights were violated, she is asked whether the procedure was explained to him, his permission obtained, and whether verbal and written consent was given for blood samples to be taken. She replies to all in the affirmative.

Quigg takes her and the jury through the injuries visible on the defendant's torso at the time of the examination as documented on the body maps that form part of the jury bundle. There are two horizontal consistent and uniform marks on the back of his legs that could have been the result of being hit with a baton or stick; a purple bruise and slight swelling on the left side of the upper back consistent with a Taser injury; multiple scratches on his upper arms; red grazing with no unbroken skin on his forehead; and dried blood and broken skin on his right knee. The nurse confirms all of these injuries were cleaned and body-mapped and that there was nothing else wrong with him, no vomiting, sweats, or pain, the suspect was alert and oriented, and the paperwork was completed and signed by them both.

The dried blood and broken skin on his right knee are in keeping with Nadine Forrester's statement that the person she saw fell to his right knee hard enough to have bruised or grazed it, but Quigg does not point this out and I wish she had. I hope the judge's assessment of the jury is correct, and that at least one of them has picked up on this small but significant detail.

Then Quigg calls to the stand the detective sergeant who carried out the taped interview with Tyson Manley. He confirms he works in the homicide division, explains for the benefit of the jury how police interviews are carried out and recorded, that he had a police constable with him throughout, and persons present also included Mr. Manley and his solicitor. Quigg asks him to read his questions aloud from the interview transcripts and says she will read the defendant's responses. She makes it clear that the parts they are reading aloud do not constitute the entirety of the interview, which lasted some eleven hours over two days, excluding breaks; repetition has been removed where the same question was asked over again, and a large number of questions that were asked and the defendant did not answer, as was his entitlement, have also been left out. The questions and answers that have been left in have been done so with the agreement of both the prosecution and the crown defense.

The particulars first: date, time commenced and concluded, and the place, that the defendant was advised he had the right if he wished to speak to his solicitor alone at any time, or to sit in silence or make no comment; just like his entitlement to kill my son then choose whether or not to take the stand and discuss it.

The first question posed by the detective sergeant relates to the fact that on March 18 a chap by the name of Ryan Williams was killed at the Sports Ground at around 18:20; did he attack this person? Quigg reads Manley's response: No.

Does he know Ryan Williams? No.

Where was he at the time the murder took place? At his girlfriend's yard.

What time did he arrive there? He'd been there since about four in the afternoon.

What was he doing there? Watching a film. Having dinner and sex.

What film did he watch? He can't remember.

Can he remember what it was about? No, he was more interested in having sex than watching the film.

Did he leave the property at any time? No, officer, definitely not.

Are there any witnesses who can corroborate his story? Sweetie Nelson was with him the whole time, she can.

On it goes. He knows nothing about the murder, wasn't there, doesn't know Ryan, has no idea if Sweetie does or why anyone would want to kill him. He's not some kind of madman. Why would he just kill someone he doesn't even know? Yes, he owned a brown sweatshirt with a gold monogram on it up until about a fortnight ago. No, it's no longer in his possession. He washed it one day and when he took it out of the machine it was ruined so he threw it out, yeah, about two weeks ago. Obviously it's not possible he could have worn it since. Did anyone see him dispose of it? He asks the detective sergeant whether he normally has a witness observe him every time he throws something in his own dustbin? What about the clothing he was wearing the day before, where is it and why isn't he wearing it now? It's at his girlfriend's house. She'd bought him the new clothing he was arrested in, and had washed the clothes he was wearing when he arrived at her house. What was it he had on? A jersey. A waistcoat. Jeans. And all of these have been washed and are at her home? Yes. As part of the package of new clothes she bought him, did Sweetie also buy him new underpants, trainers, and socks? Yes, she did. Where are his old trainers? He gave them to some homeless guy near the entrance of the estate Sweetie lives on that morning after leaving her yard to go home. The detective sergeant suggests that is very convenient. Yes, it was, Tyson Manley agrees; they had begun to stink.

Ms. Manley actually chuckles at that response. It is quiet but does not go unnoticed by me. She thinks this is humorous, her boy is funny, that his response is witty, makes him look clever. What kind of woman is she? What kind of mother? To concern herself with clothes and looking cool at her son's trial, to show up late and laughing when she must know if he's convicted he'll spend the rest of his youth behind bars. If she'd spent half as much time teaching him right from wrong as she clearly spends on her appearance, neither of us would be sitting here now. I don't realize I'm staring at her till I feel Lorna nudge my arm and I look away, blink several times, look back down at the courtroom.

As the interview is read out and Tyson Manley continues

taking the piss out of the police, my anger grows. The reading is a parody of what a sensible interview should sound like. This is the day after my son has been killed, *the following day*. He is so confident, so relaxed, joking even, having fun. I don't think he cares whether the police know he's laughing at them or not, because he doesn't care about anything. This is the boy I've been yearning would give evidence, willing him to speak to help me understand, but if this interview is anything to go by, it's probably better if he simply keeps his mouth closed. I can hardly bear to listen to this interview being read out. How much worse would it be to actually watch him stand in front of the court and speak these words himself?

He glances at his mother occasionally, whenever Quigg reads out what I assume he believes is a clever response, and though his expression is unchanged, they are sharing this, the accused and his flamboyant mother, sharing it telepathically, like I shared intimate moments of humor in the past with Ryan through eye contact, but never, ever at such an inappropriate time. In order for me to have some kind of relief, I need to see upset, I need to see Tyson Manley cry or suffer or show some indication in any shape or form that what's happened is not just one of those things of no consequence whatsoever, and I am beginning to see it will not happen. It will not happen because he just doesn't care. He killed my son and he really doesn't care at all.

I look at him sitting behind the glass gazing out. He could be any random member of the public who has popped in to watch the proceedings, a guy dragged along to the cinema to take in a film of another person's choosing, he's that disconnected. I try to imagine him as a fourteen-year-old watching his brother die. Did he exhibit emotion then? Did he weep or wail or cry? I wonder if he ever did have counseling. I study his face. No. He has had no counseling, or if he did, it was not the right kind or enough. Is that the reason my son is dead? Because no one deemed it money well spent to provide counseling for the young sibling of a person horrifically and violently slain in front of him? No one anticipated that a young person in that circumstance could not just pick up the blood-splattered pieces of his life and become a model student who would grow into an outstanding citizen? No one could anticipate that he was already in a dehumanizing spiral of violence that required intervention of some kind to break and end it? That some action needed to be taken to restore this young boy's sensibilities, to fix him?

It happens at lunchtime. The boys go off on their own and Kwame comes with Nipa, Lorna, and me to Wagamama for lunch, where we are quickly shown to a table, given our menus, and I ask Lorna to order for me because I'm bursting, then hurry to the Ladies, where I find one of the booths free. I use it, and as I exit the cubicle, she is there, bent over a sink, splashing water on her face, reviving herself, freshening up. There are only two sinks so I go to the one beside her, turn the tap on, begin to wash my hands while watching her in the mirror till she turns the tap off and looks up, and my eyes meet those of the woman whose son has killed mine. It is the first time we have been in such close proximity, alone.

I don't know if she has some kind of medical problem or smokes weed, but the whites of her eyes are intensely yellow, broken only by thin red veins. They are the kind of eyes that make people glad they've not had her life. They are tired and worn and at the same time, filled with anger. They easily add a decade to her face, and now I have seen them I understand better why she might choose to conceal them with fancy specs. For the first time I feel something akin to sympathy for this woman who has had one child taken from her violently and had to find the strength, a way to hang on, keep going, raise the living children still in her care, this woman who is no stranger to the uniqueness of the pain I bear. We inhabit a common ground, which is only crumbling around the edges because of our sons; mine is dead and hers has brought me to this pariah's place. We maintain eye contact as I wash my hands and she dries her face without speaking.

When she has finished she asks, "What?"

I have no idea of the answer, no idea what I want from her or would like her to say, or would like to say to her. I have no experience of what a person in her circumstances might think or be moved to articulate. She surely knows her son committed this act. Is it an apology I expect? If she offered one, would it make a difference?

She takes her comb out of her bag, tidies up around the edges of her hair—lucky her to still have hair left to tidy. When she finishes, she says, "There's a war going on out there. Your son was collateral damage." She puts on her sunglasses. Then leaves.

A moment later, Nipa and Lorna crash into the women's toilets in a panic, presumably having seen her as she passed them on her way out. Maybe they thought the killing gene was hereditary and that she had attacked me in the toilets. They would have been right. She did attack me, with the most powerful of weapons, words.

"Collateral damage," Lorna repeats when I tell her what Ms. Manley said. "Collateral fucking damage? What a bitch!"

6

WHEN SHE RETURNS TO THE gallery after lunch she has a young man with her who is dressed like he thinks he's a rap star. They are late and have already missed the beginning of the agreed facts, which include the coroner's report, and that at the time of his death, Ryan was carrying a knife. It was discovered at the base of his schoolbag covered in his fingerprints. It is unsheathed from the evidence bag, described as a flick knife with a ten-centimeter folding blade, and is paraded back and forth across the front of the jury box for a period of time which really isn't that long, but is nonetheless excruciating. Then there's the record of Tyson Manley's previous convictions. The convictions the jury are informed of do not include the unrelated convictions I am familiar with, the handling of stolen goods, criminal damage, loitering with intent, nor does the list include charges of which he has been acquitted in the past; possession with intent to supply. Only those convictions deemed relevant to the charges in this case are made public; possession of a class B drug, and aggra-

vated possession of a knife. Quigg works her way through
these details, bringing the prosecution case to a close. The
judge suggests a short break of fifteen minutes, and when
we return, St. Clare stands to commence the defense's case,
calling Sweetie Nelson as his first witness.

She looks tiny in the witness box, the girl without a proper
name and the brawling laugh, who gave my son the gift of
a knife and her boyfriend not only the motive to kill him
but the alibi also to cover his tracks. She is simply attired,
in a white shirt and short office skirt, like an office temp or
admin assistant, more conservatively dressed than I have ever
seen her. Her kinky afro gives her an indomitable look, but
her body language is defensive. She glances at Tyson Manley briefly. I can see no difference in his body language in
response to her though I really cannot say how much I wish I
could. Perhaps if I saw a flash of something, love, desire, pos-
sessiveness, feeling, the murder of my son might have some
point. Instead it's just more indifference, more and the same.
He killed my son not because he was enraged or jealous or
slighted; he killed him simply because he could.

I wrote a Victim Personal Statement about a month after
Ryan died. It is a document that is read out to the court after
the trial if the accused is found guilty, taken into account by
the judge before sentencing. In it I wrote about the impact
Ryan's death has had on me, on all of us, the many people
who loved my son. I struggled to find the words to explain,
wanted so desperately to make his killer know the exact
degree of devastation his death has had upon us. I talked
about Ryan in it, wanted him to be more than merely "the
deceased," wanted his murderer to know, as I did, how bright

Ryan's light burned, how gentle he was, how much he cared for others, for every living creature. I said in my statement that the killer's act took my son and changed my world. I hoped to look his killer in the eyes and read it aloud myself. In the event that I could not, the plan was for Lorna to read it on my behalf.

I should have saved myself the effort and paper. My Victim Personal Statement is only worthwhile reading to a person who has the capacity for remorse; on this defendant it is wasted. I need to speak to Nipa, find out if it can be withdrawn, if I can write another one. I have no idea what exactly I will say in it instead, just know that I could not bear to see the indifference on Tyson Manley's face as I stood there and poured my heart out. It would be like giving him my son again and I will not do that. I must remember to ask Nipa later, see what can be done.

Sweetie takes the Bible from the usher standing close by and begins to read the oath on it in a low voice, then begins again, louder this time, after the judge asks her to speak up a little and more directly into the microphone. St. Clare leads her through the essentials, her name and age and occupation; she's currently unemployed, and she gives her address reluctantly. She feels vulnerable making this information public, I can see it, and I don't really know why St. Clare thinks it necessary. She is the first of the witnesses to be asked to do this, but then she is the first witness who has been called to the stand by St. Clare.

Does she live alone? No, she lives with her mother but she's away at the moment, in rehab. She should be out soon, maybe sometime in the next month. I wonder how long her mother has been a drug addict. If her mother was taking drugs while she was pregnant she may have given birth prematurely and it would explain why Sweetie is so little. She would likely have been a small baby and her development would have been slowed if she had to go through withdrawal from whatever drugs her mother was on. It would also explain why her mother thought "Sweetie" was a good name to give her newborn daughter. But it's all supposition, as the court would say. I know nothing about her or her life, never found out much during the two short occasions I've spoken to her. For all I know, her mother was always healthy and focused one hundred percent on being a good parent. Conjecture again, but this time I doubt it. Somehow Sweetie gives the impression of a life where things have never really quite gone to plan.

St. Clare cuts to the chase fairly swiftly. Can she remember where she was on March 18?

"At home."

From when she awoke?

"I weren't feeling well. I weren't well enough to go out. I was at home the whole day."

Alone?

"Yeah."

"Where was your mother?"

"She weren't there."

"For the entire day?"

"She was in prison. On remand."

"For?"

"Soliciting."

"I see."

Never ask a question to which you do not know the answer. It's the code solicitors and barristers live by, even I know that. A barrister of his caliber would have known her answer. It doesn't add anything to his case or the alibi, except possibly to make Sweetie appear honest to a fault, but the effect it has on her is embarrassment. She looks at the jury quickly, then away. What a horrible thing to have to admit in front of a roomful of strangers. It makes me despise St. Clare a little more, and I can see it hasn't gone down well with the women in the jury either. Silly obnoxious man.

"So, on March 18, the day Ryan Williams was killed, you were at home and alone?"

"Yeah, in bed."

"And at some point during that day, Mr. Manley visited you?"

"That's right."

"Can you remember the time of day he arrived?"

"It was quarter to seven."

St. Clare, who has been slowly pacing back and forth, abruptly stops and looks directly at Sweetie. I sit forward. I am holding my breath.

St. Clare says, "I beg your pardon?"

"Quarter to seven."

"In the morning?"

"In the night."

I feel physically disoriented. The courtroom abruptly blurs then tilts before coming back upright and returning to focus. There is a rushing in my ears, impossibly the sound of my blood moving around my body more swiftly, forced to by the acceleration of my heart. I gasp, realizing the implication of Sweetie's words.

"May I remind you of the statement you made to the police on March 19—"

"I lied. Tyson told me to say he got there at four, so that's what I said."

"My Lord," St. Clare says to the judge, flustered for the first time, turning an even deeper shade of red, beet, floundering, hoping to buy more time, "This is highly irregular . . ."

"She's your witness, counsel."

There is to be no further time. St. Clare is on his own. Ms. Manley is speaking quietly but worriedly to the young man beside her. For the first time Tyson Manley has the appearance of being properly engaged in this process. He's not angry. I can't quite identify what lies behind his eyes, maybe surprise. The tension in the courtroom is palpable. The jury have shifted, are sitting up, leaning forward now, paying close attention. Sweetie has closed her eyes, locked her hands in front of her on the top of the witness box so she looks like she is praying, taking deep breaths as if to calm herself down, and I understand perfectly; it is exactly what I am doing myself.

"Yes, of course . . . thank you, My Lord. Miss Nelson, you made your statement to the police on March 19, did you not?"

She opens her eyes. "Yeah."

"I would like to hand you a copy of your statement."

"I know what I said."

"I would like to hand you a copy nonetheless. Is this a copy of the statement that you made and signed on that date?"

"Yeah."

"Do you wish to have a read of your statement to orient yourself?"

"I *know* what I said."

"So you *know*, then, that you stated on March 19, the day following the murder of Ryan Williams, while the details were still fresh and clear in your mind, that Mr. Manley visited you at your home at four p.m., and he did not leave till the following morning at eight fifteen, that you watched films and engaged in intercourse with each other till you both fell asleep, and you signed this statement declaring it to be true to the best of your belief and knowledge at that time?"

"That's what I was told to say."

"And now you are saying something different?"

"Yeah. Now, I'm telling the truth."

I can actually hear the beating of my heart. At the end of the row of seats, Ms. Manley stands. She shouts, "Liar!" and everyone in the courtroom looks up at the gallery. The young man with Ms. Manley forces her to sit back down. As soon as he releases her she is on her feet, again shouting, "Liar!" Tyson Manley stands as if about to go to his mother's aid and the guards on either side of him immediately stand too and take hold of his arms, restraining him. Sweetie looks up at the gallery. Her gaze brushes mine briefly, comes to rest near Ms. Manley, and I can't tell if her look of fear is because of Ms. Manley herself or the young man beside her. The jury watch in shock and some degree of excitement as the judge bangs his gavel repeatedly, calls for order and silence, then demands the public gallery be cleared. We are led by security out of the gallery and the door is closed behind us.

Lorna says, "Oh my God!" She is on the verge of crying. Ms. Manley and the young man with her stride purposefully toward the stairs and exit. My whole body is shaking. I cannot believe that just happened. We wait outside in the stairwell in the hope that the judge will not close the public gallery because of that outburst. About twenty minutes pass before the security guard tells us the case has been adjourned until tomorrow morning at ten.

When we leave court with Nipa and Kwame, we go to a pub nearby, where the four of us have a drink, talk about this new development and what it means. Does the case even need to continue now Tyson Manley's alibi is blown? Nipa says it does. Unless he changes his plea to guilty, the trial carries on. I cannot imagine what his defense will be if he decides to continue and let the whole thing play out.

"Well, it's obvious, isn't it?" Lorna says. "The defense is gonna have to say she's lying."

And for me, that is an enormous stress because I never trusted Sweetie, from the first time I set eyes on her, never trusted her an inch; how exactly is this jury expected to? Last night I said to Lorna the jury wouldn't believe her if it was her word against mine, and suddenly the case is hinging on them believing her over St. Clare. And that's, of course, if she actually returns, because now she has a whole night to sleep on it. If, as it appears, she's decided to come clean, it would have been better for her to have continued with her evidence today. By tomorrow morning she may have reconsidered, changed her mind. Again.

Nipa is unable to get hold of Quigg, so leaves messages on her mobile phone for her to call me back at home. Nipa says it's likely both sides are knee-deep in legal discussions. I ask her about my Victim Personal Statement, whether I can have it back, rewrite it, and she says I can't. The original Victim Personal Statement cannot be changed or withdrawn, but I can write a further statement to add to it, if I need to clarify what was written in the original or there are issues that have become apparent since the original statement was made. I say I want to do that, write a second statement, and she tells me to draft it, that she needs it by the time the defense has closed its case and she will ensure it gets to the judge in time.

Lorna and Kwame are still finishing their drinks when we leave. I'm ready to go home, want desperately to speak to Lloydie, tell him about this new development. Perhaps it will be enough to engage him, knock him off the desert island he has found for himself, back into the water, maybe to swim. It is just after three, so I ask Nipa to drop me off at the allotment, where he seems to have taken up residence. I have not been to the allotment in the last seven months, further back even, since summer last year, but it's preferable to sitting at home waiting for him to return. Perhaps on his turf, in his space, conversation will be easier. It's a good idea. I don't know why I never thought of it before.

Nipa lets me out and I enter the huge gates that separate this rural part of the city from its urban surrounds, walk the main path slowly, taking in the plots as I pass. It is so peaceful here. No wonder Lloydie comes. A few people I know, working their plots, wave or nod as I pass. They haven't seen me since the incident, and I am so familiar with the discomfort of others—their effort to be normal around me, their inability to know what normal even is with someone who carries such a grief as mine, what to say, how to say it, whether to say anything at all—that I'm sure they're glad to be halfway down their plots and able to avoid a one-to-one discussion with me entirely.

When I get to Lloydie's plot I am bewildered. I look at the adjoining plots to check that I am correct, this really is the one. His is three plots from the end, and like a child who hopes she can alter a fact, I actually count them, one, two, three, confirm that what I am looking at is undeniably his, and my confusion is replaced by a cold fear that twists my insides. The entire plot is as rigorously maintained as Kew Gardens, but there is nothing on it, not a single plant in evidence, a blade of grass, even a weed. The earth is meticulously level from the end I stand at to the top, the paths that run along the sides as clean as my kitchen floor. The herb garden is gone, the perennials, the thyme and sage and rosemary and mint, absent without a sign they ever existed. When I think about it, I can't remember the last time he brought produce home. Maybe I would have noticed earlier if I were the one doing the cooking, but Lloydie has taken over that chore completely. Looking at his plot is like looking into a void, a strip of cocoa canvas with not a single brushstroke upon it, being offered up as a completed work of art. It is an insight into his mental state that is devastating. No wonder everyone here is keeping their distance.

There is a small shed at the top, more of a shack than a shed, an outhouse built from offcuts. I walk toward it, open the rickety door, and enter. There is nothing in here that speaks of vegetation, no seeds or tubers or protected plants or crates of veg. Just his chair and his tools leaning against the wall, his rake and hoe and spade washed clean, a kettle on top of a small gas hob, some matches beside it, a tin containing tea bags, his cup, a spoon. I realize I am crying and I sit in his chair staring out through the single window overlooking this lifeless plot and try to understand just what he does all day, what it means, where this ends. He has downed tools, finished with everything, has nothing more. This is the handiwork of a man whose bags are packed and is ready to die.

I move my feet to stand and they touch something beneath the table, on the floor. I bend down, pick it up. It is a shoe box. My hands begin to shake. The act of lifting the lid is like the climax of a nightmare, the moment when horror is inevitable and, though you know it, there is nothing you can do to avoid it. Inside are a pair of football boots, Ryan's, size 11, embalmed in dark caked mud, the same ones I watched Lloydie throw out. I don't know where my head was during that time. Actually, I do know, I just don't like to go there; back to that time when Ryan's death was so new upon us and so raw, when I was consumed with rage with everyone and everything, and sought blame. Nipa brought them to the house about a month after, along with Ryan's sports bag and clothing and schoolbooks, when the forensics team had finished with them. Ryan's boots. The reason he went back. The reason he was caught alone and Tyson Manley was able to do what he did.

After Nipa left, Lloydie was sitting in the kitchen at the table, just holding them and crying. I was watching him and remembering the last time I had seen my son. Ryan's final morning had been no different from any other morning. You imagine when something like what happened to Ryan happens, perhaps that day the sky was unusually dark, mayhap the cat was hissing, the birds quiet. But it was a normal morning, ordinary, mid-March, chilly though bright with new spring sun, and the only quiet that morning came from Ryan.

I thought he was still angry with me about Sweetie, that's what I put his silence down to. He was quiet and contemplative and I thought he was punishing me. After he finished breakfast, I stood up and kissed him goodbye. It was the kiss of a parent who feels both guilty and right. Isn't that what parenting is about, feeling guilty but right? Refusing the sweets they want because you're the adult and you know too many will result in cavities? With that kiss I was trying to appease, wanted him over her and back to normal, and he accepted my kiss but did not return it, merely said goodbye. Then, as he opened the front door, Lloydie shouted to him that his football boots were still in the hallway.

"Don't forget them," he said.

And Ryan returned and packed them.

After Nipa left I watched Lloydie sobbing while crushing the boots against his chest and I was consumed with rage.

I said, "Those bloody boots! This would never have happened if you'd just kept your mouth shut!"

Then I walked out and went upstairs to the bedroom. I heard the front door open and I went to the window and watched as Lloydie threw those boots into the bin and slammed it shut. He must have returned and retrieved them afterward, has had them all this time, kept them hidden here in this sterile place. I don't touch them, can't. I replace the lid and put the box back under the table where I found it. I

brush sprinkles of mud from the table, erasing the evidence
of my presence as a child might. Finally, I stand.

It is a strange walk home, fast and driven by panic, haste
bringing me closer to a destination I am fearful of reach-
ing. Uppermost in my mind is the conversation we had last
night, the terrible words I said—yet more of them. I have to
steel myself as I put the key into the lock and turn it, open
the front door, step inside. He is not in any of the rooms
downstairs. I go upstairs, check our bedroom, the bathroom,
hesitate a moment before turning the doorknob of my son's
room and open the door. Lloydie is lying on Ryan's bed, fully
clothed, curled around Sheba, eyes closed. I walk over, stand
beside him, hold my breath, and watch his chest to see the
rise and fall of breath in this man from the life that I had
in the Before, this man that I have failed as much as he has
failed me. He stirs. Sheba awakens and stretches. His eyes
flutter open and he sits up, surprised at first, then embarrassed to be discovered in here.

"I'm sorry," he says.

I don't know what to say to him, where to begin. Instead
I sit down on the edge of the bed bedside him and kiss his
head. I cannot bring myself to mention the allotment. He has
been going there every day, seven days a week, and he has
made an effort to pretend it is for some purpose, presumably
for my sake, to protect me from the barren horror of his day-
to-day reality.

"I must have fallen asleep," he says.

I kiss him again. It feels like I've read his private diaries
behind his back and discovered in them something personal,

something so intimate it was never intended for me to see or know. And so I don't mention it, never will, just need to find a way to draw him back from the solitude and hopelessness of that place, into the light, where there is the chance for living things to survive and thrive and grow.

He says, "I don't know why I came in here."

But I know. It was to find something of his old self, the old life that has gone, to try to restore something of that time, to be close not just to his spirit but to the Ryan we loved who lived, and the people we were during that time, who seem to have vanished with our son to leave a cocoa-colored empty space. I take off my coat, sit on the bed beside him, and instead of another chaste kiss, I kiss his lips, like I have done a thousand times, slowly, lingering, a lover's kiss. Immediately he stands, flustered, like someone who has found himself on the verge of intimacy with the wrong person. He runs his hands over the shock of his grief-bleached hair.

"I need to start dinner," he says, "I'm sorry," and leaves me with Sheba on the bed. It smells of Lloydie in here, of Ryan when he helped himself to his father's aftershave, like a delicious memory springboarding a current event. I am afraid to tell him about Sweetie, afraid to bring him face-to-face with what he is avoiding most. I don't know what to do for the best, whether pushing him too hard is likely to send him over the edge of the precipice he's so precariously balanced on. My ignorance as to how to best help him overwhelms me, makes me feel helpless, and in the end I do what has become habit now: nothing. I pour myself a drink and run a bath.

Don't discuss Ryan. Don't bring up the case. Don't talk about Sweetie. Don't mention the allotment. I talk about the dinner

Lloydie has cooked as we eat at the table in the kitchen. This is where the return lies, in normalcy, the doing of the things we used to do, in refusing to allow the cowardice of avoidance to set the terms. I talk about the food and we speak about Rose and Dan and I sit at the table with my husband and ignore his discomfort, the awkwardness that has become a feature of his body language when it's just us two alone. I'm sure he's relieved at the end of it when I finish and leave him downstairs, go up on my own to our bed.

I ring my mother, speak to Leah, then Quigg, and afterward call Lorna on her landline at home. She doesn't answer, and I have already started dialing her mobile number when it occurs to me she may be sleeping. I put the phone down. I don't want to wake her if she's having an early night. My life, this case, it's enough to knock the stuffing out of anyone. I put the TV in the bedroom on instead and stare at the colors while I wait for my regular nighttime combo to take effect.

The next morning, there is a cup of tea on the side and I take it downstairs and drink it, sipping slowly and watching Lloydie tidy the already clean counters, wipe out the spotless interior of the fridge. He does the tiny pile of washing-up hurriedly, then leaves before Nipa arrives, and I cannot think of where he's heading or I'll cry.

We are first into the public gallery as always, take our regular seats at the end of the front row. There is an air of excitement in the courtroom that is palpable and appears to have everyone, apart from the accused, in its grip. Even Ms. Manley appears to have been able to get out of bed when the alarm went off this morning. She is punctual for the first time,

alone, wearing her signature sunglasses, sitting on her customary seat at the farthest end of the front row.

The judge gives us another telling off before the case com-
mences. He tells us if we cannot contain ourselves, if there are
any further outbursts or disturbances, he will have the gallery
cleared. Whereas normally the security guards merely pass in
and out as needed, today, one of them remains inside the gallery once the case gets under way. I take this as a sign the judge
means business, and hope Ms. Manley has noted this and
behaves herself; while she probably visits many courts, attending lots of cases, so being chucked out of this one might not be
such a big deal for her, this is the only one I've ever attended,
and it is vitally important to me I see it through.

The judge reiterates what Quigg told me last night on the
phone, that St. Clare has made an application for Sweetie to
be treated as a hostile witness. I think about those two girls
at the café, her terror when she saw them, and I feel sick. I'm
desperate with the hope that her resolve has not weakened
overnight and with the anticipation of listening to her evidence if it hasn't. But I am also scared, on her behalf, sick
and scared. St. Clare will do everything he can to destroy her
credibility as a witness, and once he's finished with her and
she leaves this courtroom, her exit will mark the beginning
of an entirely new set of problems. I told her she could make
choices, and now that she has, I feel responsible for what is
about to unfold.

When she is called to the stand, she steps inside the witness box nervously. She looks extremely tired, as though last
night she managed hardly any sleep. She is wearing the same
outfit she had on yesterday, but it is a little grubby, a bit more
creased with wear, and I can't help but feel that her appear-

ance makes worse what is already a position of serious disadvantage. The young man who was with Ms. Manley yesterday arrives. Ms. Manley moves her bag and he takes his seat beside her. He is wearing large designer sunglasses as well, and instead of support, he looks like part of her entourage.

St. Clare stands as he did with Kwame, hands buried deep in his pockets as if butter wouldn't melt in his mouth. He is immaculately dressed and shod, but looking a little worse for wear himself, probably from the liquor he was knocking back last night while trying to get his head around how exactly he was going to front this case. He reminds Sweetie that she is under oath and has sworn to tell the truth before he begins, speaking slowly and putting an emphasis on his words that leaves no doubt in anyone's mind he's of the opinion she's come to court with the full intention of lying her head off. She glares at St. Clare as a hostile witness might. I can't decide whether her anger is better than the nervousness it has replaced, but it appears to bolster her confidence. As St. Clare speaks, the resilience of the woman with the kinky afro seems to grow.

He begins by asking her about her relationship with Tyson. She has been seeing him for about three years.

"So the defendant has been your boyfriend continuously for all of that time?"

Sweetie answers, "I wouldn't exactly class him as a boyfriend."

"May I ask what you *would* class him as?"

"We link up from time to time, that's it."

"When you say you 'link up,' you mean you meet specifically for intercourse with each other?" St. Clare says.

"Yeah."

"Do you ever go out on dates, to the movies for example, or to restaurants for meals?"

"No."

"So your entire relationship revolves around meeting for intercourse?"

"I s'pose."

"Is that a yes?"

"Yeah, yes."

"Yesterday, you told the court that the reason you gave a statement to the police on March 19 stating that Mr. Manley arrived at your house on March 18 at 4 p.m. was because he had told you to lie about the time he arrived."

" 'S right."

"That seems a rather unlikely thing to do for someone with whom you are not in a relationship."

"Well, I never exactly had a choice."

"Really? Would you tell the court why you felt you had no choice other than to take actions which could well be deemed to have perverted the course of justice?"

A pause, then, "I was scared."

"Of what?"

Sweetie glances at Tyson Manley. "Him."

"Of Mr. Manley?"

"Yeah."

"At the time you made your statement, were you aware Mr. Manley was being questioned about a murder?"

"Yeah."

"You were aware that a person found guilty of murder would likely be sentenced to a prison term?"

"Yeah."

"And knowing this person you claim to be scared of might go to prison, you thought the best thing would be to lie and by so doing, ensure he remained free?"

"That weren't exactly how I thought about it."

"Would you be so kind as to tell the court exactly how you did think about it?"

"I just . . . y'know . . . he told me what to say and I said it."

"Even though he was not your boyfriend or someone with whom you were in a relationship?"

"Yeah."

"Can you really expect the court to believe that?"

Sweetie's voice is raised as she replies, "Look, you're the one asking what happened! I'm just tryin'a tell you."

St. Clare does not acknowledge her annoyance. His own tone is unchanged. "Miss Nelson, if, as you claim, you were afraid of Mr. Manley, would it not have made more sense for you to have said he was *not* with you, thus increasing the likelihood of his going to prison?"

It makes no difference whether she is rude to St. Clare or not. He is patiently relentless, will not stop or back off. Sweetie stops fidgeting, looks down. I don't see it, but I imagine she sighs. "Y'know, it ain't just him, he's got his crew." Her gaze flicks upward to the gallery briefly, to the man beside Ms. Manley.

"You mean his friends?"

"Yeah."

"So now you're afraid of him *and* his friends?"

Judging from her expression, she knows exactly how he's trying to make her look here. "Yeah, I'm afraid of him *and* his friends."

"I see. Just how many close friends would you say Mr. Manley has?"

"Four. There's others, but close ones, four."

"And these four friends, are they not your friends also?"

"No, they ain't my friends."

"Do excuse me, but I must be clear on this point; these four people whom you say are not your friends, how many of them have you had intercourse with?"

Sweetie doesn't answer. She looks at the judge. He does not help her. There is no one in the room on her side to stop St. Clare from going too far. It's normally the job of the barrister on the other side to say, "I object! It is entirely inappropriate for the witness to be questioned in this fashion, Your Honor." But Quigg isn't here for Sweetie. No one is. The question is repeated. Her shoulders slump. Her voice when she answers is low.

"I'm sorry?" St. Clare asks, though I heard her response in the public gallery, so I'm sure everyone in the courtroom did as well. "Did you say *all* of them?"

"Yeah."

"Yet you maintain they are not your friends?"

"They ain't my friends."

"I see. Miss Nelson, how old is your baby?"

I shake my head, imagine I have misheard the question till Sweetie answers, "Two weeks."

"And still in the hospital?"

"Yeah. She was early. And small. So they kept her in."

I look at her breasts again. They are much larger than they were before. But other than that, she is carrying no pregnancy weight whatsoever. Her body bears no other indication she has recently given birth. That's why I missed it. And it all makes sense now, her tiredness, why she's wearing the same grubby outfit. Presumably she's come directly from the hospital today. Her mother's in rehab. Perhaps she has no one looking out for her, washing her clothes, bringing her a decent meal; Sweetie's a mother.

"And who is the father of your child?" St. Clare is patient, brushes something from the front of his robe, gives her time before prompting, "Miss Nelson; the father?"

Finally Sweetie answers, "I don't know."

"I see. What about Mr. Manley. Could it be him?"

"Yeah."

"These four people whom you say are not your friends, could it be any of them?"

"Yeah."

"The deceased, Ryan Williams, might he be the father of your child?"

My heart begins to accelerate. Sweetie glances at Tyson quickly, looks away, downward. "Yeah."

Now it is thudding inside my chest. Lorna says, "Oh my God!"

"It could, in fact, be any of them?"

"Yeah."

I have a list in my mind of things my son never did, ordinary things people normally do during their lifetime, many of them things they probably took for granted, of no special note, hardly treasured experiences, regular things like he never drove a car, never cooked a meal, never visited Paris, got married, passed a GCSE or an A level, or skied. He never raved all night or got properly drunk, opened a bank account or left home. It is infinite the number of things his life was never long enough for him to do. Never had sex was on that list, and never had children.

The hope that is ignited inside my chest is like an electric shock. Seven months of despair and suddenly my heart is pounding, alive with the possibility that her baby might be my grandchild, Ryan's daughter. I try to talk myself down, think reasonably, be logical—*Why would it be his? She's clearly slept with everyone. The odds are better getting a winning line on the lottery than her baby being my son's*—but it is a hope that is impossible to diminish that easily. I do the maths. The dates work. My son was seeing her. This really could be.

Lorna takes my hand, whispers, "Calm down." Her grip is so tight she's crushing my fingers.

Quigg finally stands, "My Lord, I am having difficulty understanding where my learned friend is heading with his line of questioning. It is probably my own lack of understanding. It would, however, be very helpful if he would make it clear."

The Judge asks, "Counsel, is this leading to a relevant point?"

"I assure you, My Lord, it is. I ask you to permit me some latitude, and the purpose of these questions shall shortly become clear."

"I hope they do, and swiftly," the judge says.

"Thank you, My Lord. Is it not the case, Miss Nelson, that you visited Mr. Manley at Feltham Young Offenders' Institute three weeks ago, and that you argued with him about your baby and who the father was?"

"Yeah, I visited him."

"And you argued. Specifically, Mr. Manley advised you that you did not have his permission to put him down on the birth certificate as the father of your child?"

Sweetie doesn't answer, doesn't need to. The question seems to physically deflate her.

St. Clare pushes, "That is the truth, is it not?"

"Yeah, but . . ."

"Miss Nelson, I put it to you that Mr. Manley *did* arrive at your home on March 18 at four p.m., and that the statement you made to the police on March 19 stating this was in fact true. I put it to you that because you had no idea who the father of your child was, you hoped to legitimize her by having Mr. Manley, with whom you had been having intercourse on and off for a period of at least three years, put his name on the birth certificate as her father. I submit that his refusal to do this—and I shall leave it to others to judge whether this decision was reasonable or not—upset you a great deal, in fact it made you extremely angry. The truth is that you have changed your story now about the time he arrived at your home, *not* because you have decided to tell the truth, but because you want revenge?"

Sweetie looks as though she is close to tears. She shakes her head. " 'S not true."

St. Clare says, "I have no further questions."

Then something truly hideous happens. A patch begins to grow on Sweetie's blouse at the site of her left breast. It is wet and the moisture makes the thin cotton transparent as it spreads, so that the lacy detail of her bra becomes visible. Another patch begins on the right. She is younger than Leah by a year, this girl before the court whose baby is in the hospital and whose milk is leaking, and she is mortified with embarrassment, ineffectually tries to raise her handbag, her hands, to cover herself, to preserve some dignity here where there is none to be found. Lorna begins to cry, gets up, walks out of the public gallery, stumbling past us, bumping the legs of Ms. Manley, still seated at the end of the row.

Quigg stands and asks for an adjournment, to which the judge agrees, and the security guard directs everyone in the gallery to leave as well. Lorna is standing at the top of the stairs, trying to compose herself. I touch her arm. She shakes her head, cannot speak.

Nipa says, "Let's go outside, get some air," and we go down the stairs and outside, where Lorna pulls off her jacket and her cardigan, hands the cardigan to Nipa.

"Please, please give this to her. She can keep it. I don't want it back."

We go with Nipa to the court reception, wait at the desk as she goes through security, disappears up the stairs.

"This is terrible," Lorna says. "Terrible! That poor, poor girl."

And it is awful. It is the worst thing I can imagine that could happen to any new young mum on the stand. But most new mums would not be on the stand. Most new mums with a two-week-old baby in the hospital would be at the hospital, beside the cot. And as bad as I feel for her and what has just happened, it is secondary to the hope, as unlikely as the chances are; can it really be possible that Sweetie Nelson has given birth to Ryan's child?

The first time I met Sweetie, that very first time, the thought of her being the mother of my grandchild was abhorrent to me. I have been trying to understand Ryan's death, why it happened, what it was he ever did that he should die the way he died, but if there was some purpose or meaning to it, perhaps it was meant to be a lesson not for him, but for me, maybe the taking of my son was meant to teach *me* something, a lesson of such magnitude, one I had no idea I needed to learn: humility. I have gone from abhorrence at the idea of Sweetie bearing Ryan's child to it being the greatest thing I could ever wish for, the gift of life from this girl I deemed so low, the continuation of my son's line, the infinity of future generations bearing his genes.

I need to keep calm. That baby may not be his at all, probably isn't. And yet there is a chance, the smallest, remotest, unlikeliest chance, and it flickers in my chest like a beacon.

7

WE HAVE SHIFTED, LORNA AND I. I feel it when we are back in the public gallery, when we are looking down at Sweetie on the witness stand wearing Lorna's cardigan, buttoned to the top and slightly too large. Somehow I am stronger. Where it has come from exactly I cannot say, but it is to do with hope, it is to do with light, it is to do with energy I have not felt for at least seven months that has given me a supercharge. Lorna holds a tissue at the ready in one hand and I hold her other hand in mine. Ms. Manley sits in the second seat from the end of the row, beside the young man accompanying her, face forward, back erect.

The judge asks Sweetie, "Would you rather sit to give your evidence?"

She nods. "Yeah, I would."

He directs a clerk to bring a chair for her to sit on, and while this is being done, he advises Sweetie to let him know if it becomes too much or if she wishes to have a break. She says she will and thanks him. Every time I have ever looked at her before she has seemed older than her years, too grown-up for my liking. This is the first time I have looked at her and seen her for what she is, a woman who has given birth, and at the same time, little more than a child.

Quigg begins scene-setting, starting with Sweetie's relationship with Tyson Manley. I don't know whether the jury have been studying her as closely as I have throughout this trial, whether she seems less confident to them as well, more tentative, probably because she doesn't know all the answers in advance. I think it makes her seem warmer, more human, and the result is that Sweetie's responses to her are less defensive than her responses were to St. Clare, more open and full. Sweetie tells the court she lives in a small block of flats around the corner from Tyson's home. She had friends who lived on his estate that she spent time with outside of school. A few of them had been involved with Vito, the elder brother, were part of a shifting group that hung out together there. Her friends always teased her about Tyson fancying her, but she had just laughed it off, because he was simply Vito's kid brother. Up until Vito got shot, they were just friends. Afterward, Sweetie says, everything changed, including Tyson. He was filled with anger. There were all manner of rumors circulating about who had shot Vito and why, and the fact the police seemed to treat the investigation as if it were a low priority did nothing to help. Over a short time Tyson went from being almost a cheeky younger brother to not knowing what to believe or whom he could trust. Her biggest mistake was thinking that maybe with her influence, she could keep him on the right track. Though she doesn't actually say the words, I think she felt sorry for him.

" 'S like he was tryin'a be an older when he was just still a younger, and 'cause of that, he had to be harder. Like anything nice made him look weak and he was determined no one was gonna think he was weak. Yeah, I was stupid, I thought we was gonna be tight. I'm not saying wifey or nothing, but 's like he went from being my friend to only sleeping with me when he wannid, like that was all I was good for. I thought it was gonna be more. Yeah, he bought me stuff, gave me money and that, but I didn't wanna just end up being some stupid crackhead ho. I know it sounds lame, but I really cared about him and I wannid him to care about me back, and Tyson never, he never did. But even though he just wannid to link with me, 's like somehow he owned me, like no one else was supposed to check me, even though he weren't really checking me hisself. Twenty-four seven, him and his man-dem was grilling me, what I did and where I went, who I spoke to, what for, and by the time I realized I wannid out, it was too late."

"Couldn't you just have told Mr. Manley you no longer wished to have this relationship with him?"

"You don't tell someone like Tyson that you don't wanna be with them then just go home. And I never had nowhere to go except home. I'da been finished."

"When you say 'finished,' what exactly do you mean? What would have happened?"

"I can't tell you things I've seen, things I know man's done to girls. I doubt you'd even believe me. Let's just say it wouldn'a been good."

"Miss Nelson, is it true you were seeing the deceased, Ryan Williams, that you had a relationship with him of some kind?"

"Yeah."

"Can you tell us about that relationship? Were you boyfriend and girlfriend?"

"I wouldn't exactly class us as boyfriend and girlfriend; we were friends, good friends. He asked me out. That's no big thing to you probably, but no one ever asked me out before. I was used to man telling me what I was gonna do, when and how. When he asked me out, it's like I had a choice. I never chose nothing before in my life that wasn't some shit choice between one bad thing and the next worse . . . sorry, I shouldn't have said 'shit,' should I?"

"Probably not. But please go on. You were explaining about your relationship with Ryan Williams, that when he asked you out, it felt like you were able to make a choice."

"Yeah. But I was scared as well 'cause Tyson never wannid me seeing no one. I knew from day one the whole thing woulda ended in some kinda beef, so I told Ryan no, but it never made no difference. He wasn't in my face or nothing, he just kept asking and I just kept saying no, and it was like the more I said no, the more he asked me. He was a nice guy, really sweet, and I wannid that, just one good thing that I wannid and got to pick myself. So one day I just said yeah. I never said I'd be his girl or nothing, I just said we'd go out and see how it went."

"So you went on a date with Ryan?"

"Yeah. He took me to Kentucky. Bought me a Meal Deal. He talked to me, proper talked, and listened. I never had no one ever wanna listen to me before, and he weren't even tryin'a get down my knickers or nothing, I mean I know he was hoping, but it was more than just that. He wasn't using me or cussing me or dissing me, he really liked me, and even though I never meant to, I started liking him back. But it was like the more I liked him, the scareder I got, 'cause I didn't know how it could work, y'know? Anyway, in the end I called it off, I said we couldn't meet no more, 'cause I was used to the way them man-dem done things and I could deal with whatever went down, but Ryan wasn't on that level, and I was scared what would happen if it came out."

"Can you tell me when you called it off with Ryan, was it days before he was killed? Weeks? Months?"

"About three weeks before. At school. I told him I didn't wanna see him no more, said he was just a youth, a boy, that I didn't give a sh— . . . never had no feelings for him. I told him to leave me alone, but he never. He wouldn't stop calling me and texting, and he said he knew I had feelings for him and he weren't gonna stop till I told him the truth. So I did, told him about Tyson and me, and he still never stopped. He said I deserved better. Me. He said, 'Every single creature in the world is entitled to happiness.'" Sweetie laughs. It is a sad laugh. "Those are the exact words he said."

My son, the champion of worms, the liberator of spiders, of course that's what he said to Sweetie. Maybe he would have grown up to become a fireman or counselor or doctor. He was destined to rescue, save lives. Her helplessness would have made him stick his heels in, her plight would have brought to the fore everything within him that was decent and strong and optimistic. She was vulnerable and he would never have turned his back on her, would never have washed his hands clean and walked away, would never have abandoned this girl, especially, as I think is clear for the courtroom to see, especially when it was obvious how much she cared about him.

"Miss Nelson, did Mr. Manley find out you had been seeing Ryan?"

"Yeah. Ryan rang when Tyson was at my yard one night. I ignored it. I never put Ryan in my contacts 'cause Tyson and his crew was always checking my phone and I made sure I deleted all our texts and that, but the phone rang and Tyson was there and Ryan left a message and Tyson took my phone and listened to it."

"Do you remember the date that happened?"

"It was March 17."

"What happened next?"

Sweetie glances at Tyson nervously. He is watching her with an expression that sits somewhere between menace and mockery. I glance at Ms. Manley at the end of the row. The woman is a robot. I'm sure she is sitting exactly as she was the last time I looked. My eyes return to Sweetie. She is squeezing her hands together, realizes, stops. Perhaps to keep them still, she clasps the top of the witness box hard.

"He said I was fuckry bitch, called me a sket."

"A sket?"

"A ho. He said he was gonna deal with us."

"Mr. Manley said this to you?"

"Yeah."

"When he said he would 'deal' with you, what did you take that to mean?"

"*Deal* with us. Hurt us, innit."

"Both you and Ryan?"

"Yeah."

"How did you respond to that?"

"We was arguing and I was tryin'a tell him it weren't nothing, then one of his man-dem rung him 'cause someone got shanked . . ."

"Shanked?"

"Stabbed. Tyson put his clothes on and went."

"What happened next?"

"I wannid to ring Ryan and warn him, but Tyson still had my phone, so I went to his house . . ."

"Ryan Williams's home?"

"Yeah. I told him Tyson knew about us, that he had to watch his back. I gave him a knife, told him to keep it for protection. Tyson wouldn'a felt no way about shanking Ryan, I knew that. I don't know if Ryan thought I was exaggerating or what, 'cause he just kept telling me not to worry. Then he said I could stay at his if I wannid."

"And what did you reply?"

"I said no. I'd already met his mum and I knew she never liked me. I didn't blame her. If he was my son, I wouldn'a wannid him mixed up with someone like me; it's not like I didn't get it. I said I was cool, that he needed to worry about hisself. Then his mum called him in and I walked around a bit but there wasn't nowhere to go, so I went back home."

"This was still the evening of March 17?"

"Yeah."

"You're sure of the date?"

"That was the last time I saw Ryan. I'd never forget that date."

"Thank you. So you went back home . . ."

"No."

"I'm sorry?"

"I *was* gonna go back home, but I got mugged."

"On the way home?"

"Yeah."

"Mugged?"

Sweetie is quiet for a moment, nods her head, glances at Tyson Manley briefly then down at her lap. Her voice is low. "Yeah. My bag got stole. They broke my nose, had to be reset, you can still see the mark . . ." She lifts her head, touches the raised ridge on the bridge of her nose, puts her hand back down. " . . . I'll probably always have it. The hospital kept me in overnight."

Quigg says, "I see."

I feel sick. It is the glance that did it, achieved the seemingly impossible, evoked a response from Tyson Manley for a second only, shifted the indifference in his eyes to a coldness I would not expect to see in the eyes of a child, a seventeen-year-old boy. His expression returns to indifference again so quickly it is hard to believe such a coldness was ever there at all. But it was, and I caught it. She wasn't mugged at all; he did it. I don't know why Sweetie doesn't say that. But if I caught that glance, it's likely Quigg did too. I wait for her to pick up on it, but after a pause Quigg says, "So the day before Ryan Williams was murdered, you were the victim of a robbery?"

"Yeah."

"You sustained injuries?"

"Yeah."

"You went to the hospital, where you were treated and kept in overnight?"

"Yeah."

"And the following day, you were discharged?"

"Yeah."

"Can you remember what time that was?"

"In the morning, about ten."

I realize I have been holding my breath, release it, trying to understand why Quigg has simply let it go. I have to trust that she knows what she is doing, even though I don't.

"So you got home at what time?"

"Musta been eleven."

"And you were at home, alone, from eleven until Mr. Manley came around?"

"Yeah."

"What time did he arrive?"

"Quarter to seven, in the night."

"And you let him in?"

"He came in, he never asked."

"Can you remember what he was wearing?"

"A brown sweat top, black jogging bottoms, Nike trainers."

St. Clare appears absorbed in the details of the folder open on the table in front of him. He does not look up as Quigg shows Sweetie the photograph of Tyson Manley lifted from his Facebook page, asks, "Miss Nelson, is this the top Mr. Manley was wearing?"

Sweetie says, "Yeah."

"Thank you." Quigg addresses the judge. "My Lord, I'm aware it is almost one o'clock now. This may be a convenient moment for the court to break for lunch."

The judge finishes the note he is writing, looks up. "Thank you, counsel. I believe it is."

I ask Nipa to give us some space over lunch and I head with Lorna and Kwame to the pub we ate at on the first day of the trial. As soon as we are out in the fresh air, Lorna says, "You know the chances of that baby being Ryan's are slim to none, don't you?"

"They're just slim, aren't they?"

"You tell me. Do *you* think Ryan slept with her?"

I think about Sweetie squirming on my son's lap, my fear of leaving them alone together the first time I met her, feel the hope rising. "It's possible."

Kwame asks, "Why would she make it up?"

"I don't know," I say.

"Maybe she's still looking for a father to stick on the birth certificate. That could be a motive," Lorna says.

"Even if she did sleep with Ryan, she also slept with at least five other guys around the same time," I say; not one or two, *five*. Not just my son and Tyson Manley in a kind of love triangle that would make some sense of my son's murder, but loads of guys; loads. This is the caliber of the love of my son's too short life.

Inside the busy packed pub, we loiter close to a couple who look as though they are on the verge of vacating, grab their table the moment they do. There is a large group gathered around a couple of tables beside us, suited men and women in stilettos, celebrating something, a birthday or victory of some kind. They are unaffected, loud, and laughing frequently in the parallel universe that exists alongside ours.

"I'm surprised Quigg didn't ask more about Sweetie's mugging," Kwame says.

"I think you mean her so-called mugging," Lorna says. "What a huge coincidence. Tyson's furious with her, enough for her to warn Ryan and give him a knife, then that same evening she's badly beaten enough to be admitted to the hospital. What are the chances of it being completely random?"

"Those chances are the ones that are slim to none," I say. "But why do you think she didn't just say it?"

Kwame says, "Maybe she was scared? Maybe it would implicate more people than just Tyson Manley."

I feel sick just thinking about it, try to prevent my imagination from going there, from visualizing a group of boys beating that tiny girl on the stand, maybe more than just beating her, worse.

"I was thinking about Fimi," Lorna says. "When Sweetie was giving her evidence, thinking about Fimi telling us her son was killed because of a look he gave someone, thinking about Ryan being killed 'cause he fancied the wrong girl."

"It's insane," Kwame says. "Pure madness."

Lorna says, "I don't know, this generation of boys, we've failed them completely."

I will not accept the blame for Tyson Manley, for the deplorable things he has done. I say, "*We?* There is no *we* in this. It's slack parenting, nothing more, parents not doing their job properly. Blame the mother."

"Marce, that woman was out of her depth. I don't know if she ever had everything in place to be a great mum in the first place, but it seems to me that even if she did, her life would've knocked it out of her."

"Why're we even talking about her?" Kwame asks. "What about his dad? Where was Vito's dad, Tyson's dad? Have you seen him in the public gallery? Two people conceived that boy, brought him into the world. Where the hell's the other one?"

It strikes me as extraordinary that I've never given Tyson Manley's father a thought before, just accepted his complete absence without question. Maybe he's a conservationist. Maybe he's in Borneo this very second, working to protect some indigenous rain forest tribe from extinction. Perhaps that was what he and Ms. Manley had in common when they met. He is obviously not around now, has obviously massively failed his son, but I think about Ms. Manley, her cool shades and overpowering perfumes. His absence is not enough to exempt her from blame. Look at Lorna, Leah. "It *is* possible to be a good single parent," I say.

"It's easier to be a single parent raising girls," Kwame says. "Girls take their role models from their mums, the nursery staff, teachers, dinner ladies, the school nurse, their child minder. They're surrounded by women from birth. But if you're on your own and your boys are heading off track . . ." He shakes his head. "Some of these boys, their first serious interaction with adult males is when they get expelled or in trouble with the police. They need their dads before they get to that point."

"In an ideal world," Lorna says. "But these kids aren't living in an ideal world. I thought it was pretty wretched when Sweetie was saying she liked Ryan not because they had the same sense of humor or masses of things in common, but because he was the first person who was interested in her. I mean, how tragic is that?"

Kwame shakes his head. "It's a killer."

"You never really think about those kids who've never had anyone in their life interested in them, not one single person," she says.

"Loads of the boys I work with, no one cared about them till they bucked up on other boys no one cared about," Kwame says. "No one does anything till they've completely gone off the rails. Suddenly there's no end of resources, for court costs and solicitors, PRUs, detention centers, prison, you name it."

Lorna says, "You're right. By the time they've got our attention, it's already too late. We're just too selfish, all of us, too busy and selfish to care."

"Some of us *are* trying to make a difference," Kwame says, and for a moment he is illuminated in my mind, Kwame the football coach, teaching his young men a thousand things other than how to correctly kick a ball.

"Some," Lorna says, "but not enough,"

They're right. I kept my little family safe. I concerned myself with me and the people closest to me. I read about young people, crime, knives, gangs, guns, killings over nonsense, but they were nothing to do with the tiny safe haven I thought I'd created to insulate myself and mine. I have never done a single thing in my life for anyone like Tyson Manley or Sweetie. I've given money to help refugees and political prisoners abroad, paid monthly standing orders to the Red Cross, Sight Savers, Amnesty International. I've made donations by text when I've been on trains and seen posters; for child brides in third world countries whose wombs and lives are devastated as a result of giving birth too young; to eradicate polio in Nigeria and Afghanistan. I've made one-off payments by debit card to hurricane and tsunami and Ebola appeals, and here at home across the way from where I live, there are children bringing themselves up, responsible for managing their time when they are excluded from school and society, getting involved in crime because there is nothing else to do, carrying knives because in their world it is the only way to overcome an aggressor who has a problem with you, asks no questions, and carries a knife too; children being shot, stabbed, living in fear, and not only have I never given a penny or a minute of my time to make a difference, but the thought has never even crossed my mind. The only reason I'm even thinking about it now is because that underworld out there has crashed in irrevocably on my own. If it hadn't, I would still be oblivious now.

"What do you think will happen to Sweetie?" I ask. "And

the baby?" That little girl whose odds against her being my grandchild are stacked so high.

"I don't know," Lorna says. "I was gonna speak to Nipa about her, whether anyone's working with her. She's brave, but she's in deep shit. I can't imagine she can go back home. I'm gonna speak to Nipa, make sure she doesn't slip through the so-called safety net . . ."

"Or worse, next time we hear about her is on the news," Kwame says. "Those people she's dealing with aren't jokers."

"I'll speak to Nipa today," Lorna says, "Make sure something's done, someone knows she exists and needs help."

"And if we can see her, see the baby, make sure they're okay," I say. I don't add *so we can see if her tiny face bears any resemblance to my son's*, but I think it.

That evening I saw her standing outside the front door, in the garden speaking to Ryan, I watched them from my bedroom window, kept the light off so I wouldn't be seen, went so far as to close the door to extinguish any silhouette that might be cast by the passage light. I thought he had broken up with her and she had come to beg him to change his mind; that's how it looked. She was clearly upset, very emotional, and Ryan was so calm, talking down whatever she was saying with his youthful logic. I imagined he was saying, "I need to concentrate on my studies. We had a good time, Sweetie, but it's over now. I'm sorry. I never meant to hurt you." Instead she was giving him a knife to protect himself, and my son, so trusting, *too* trusting, Sweetie said, was taking it, promising her he'd keep it close. All those talks we'd had, the things I'd sheltered him from, all so that we, Lloydie and I, would be the greatest influence on his childhood and future, all those discussions and he still took the knife she gave him, had it on him the day he died. If only I had seen it from the window as I watched, but I wasn't looking out for knives. My focus was on Ryan's resolve. My worry was that if she carried on, he might weaken, give in, and agree to go out with her again. That was my biggest fear the day before he died, the worst thing I could imagine, that my son might make the decision to go out with someone I didn't like. So naïve. So naïve.

So I went downstairs, opened the front door, and called him in, stood there allowing them no further time together, waited for him to come inside and her to leave. I feel a quickening in my stomach, swallow another glassful of wine to settle it. When I drove her from my front door, I never gave her welfare a thought. Now I'm being forced to, and it's too much.

"This is all my fault," I say, and hear in my voice the quaver of the closeness of tears.

"Rubbish," says my sister. "It bloody well isn't."

"I don't even know if it's helpful for me to say this," Kwame says, "but once Tyson felt dissed it was always gonna end bad. Whether he killed Ryan that day or the following one or the next week, whether it was at the Sports Ground or the playground or the library, that boy is so damaged and angry, only thing that would've stopped him is if someone killed him first or he got locked up for something else, and even then he would have passed time planning to kill Ryan when he came out. He doesn't think like me or you. Once he made the decision, nothing you could've done would've changed it."

I was his mother. It was my job to see Ryan safely through to adulthood. That was my job and I failed. There must have been something more I could have done.

"There's me buying him PlayStation and Wii," I say. "I should've been spending that money on karate, teaching him how to use a bow, given him boxing lessons, knuckle dusters . . ."

"Taught him to hurt? To hate instead of trust?" Lorna asks. "Yeah, he would have been quite some nephew then."

"I just don't understand why he took it, that knife, why he was carrying it; I don't understand."

"Marce, you're never gonna know. Maybe he didn't wanna leave it in the house in case you found it. Maybe he carried it because he was scared. Maybe he forgot he had it on him. It was at the bottom of his rucksack, not stuck in his waistband. It was an error of judgment. Everyone's allowed an error of judgment. It doesn't mean anything."

But she's wrong of course, because it means everything. If he was scared enough to carry it, he was scared enough to discuss it with me, and maybe he would have if I'd left that doorway open instead of doing what I did, marching in all guns blazing and telling him what to do.

I feel guilty. My son is dead and I feel guilty. There were opportunities that I missed and I feel guilty. That's what I should have asked Fimi when I had the chance; as a parent of a child who has been violently killed, is it possible, ever, to completely absolve yourself of blame?

We wait on the stairwell outside the doorway that leads to the public gallery entrance for about fifteen minutes before we are permitted back into the courtroom after lunch. Ms. Manley is sitting on her own in the corner seat of the front row, the guy who was with her this morning nowhere in sight, and although it's perfectly reasonable I suppose, he's perfectly entitled to choose what he does and where and for how long, because of Sweetie's evidence this morning, his absence feels ominous.

Ms. Manley's expression is indifference with a touch of attitude, just like her son's. There is nothing in her bearing of humility or embarrassment, no indication that listening to the details of this trial has been unsettling for her, raised any questions about her parenting approach, made her wonder whether maybe somewhere along the way, possibly she could have done something wrong. It is the same indifference I have been observing in her son. What if one of her children had been a daughter? Would she have seen things differently then? Would she still have thought it okay for her son to use women and call them whores? I glance over at her, watch her uncross her legs then cross them again, adjust her posture, trying to get comfy. It wouldn't have made a difference. Ryan didn't have any sisters. Either you know right from wrong or you don't.

I wonder how they are together, the mother and son. Sixteen years of age and Ryan still liked to snuggle up beside me when we were home passing an evening, watching a film. Lloydie always ended up in the single chair, apart. I would sit at one end of the settee and Ryan took up the rest of the space, lying across it with his head on my lap and Sheba in close proximity, a living body-warmer sprawled across his feet or behind his legs, or stretched out lengthways on the settee in front of him so he could stroke her while I stroked his hair. Did Ms. Manley ever do that with her boys? It seems unbreachable, the space between an evening passed that way and killing someone simply because they've pissed you off.

Then Sweetie is called in and she enters and takes her place in the witness box. She looks exhausted, which I'm sure she must be. I have no idea how much sleep she's been getting, how much support she has by night while she and the baby are at the hospital. Even if she'd had a straight week's worth of sleep, this has been a very grueling morning for her. If it were me, having made it through the morning session, I wouldn't have wanted to return. I would've been tempted to do a runner over the lunch break. But here she is, back and facing the court. She's brave, this girl, and strong. I hope her strength extends beyond this room, to the world outside it she is going to have to face.

Tyson is as he always is, appearing disengaged but not taking his eyes off Sweetie, who I think has steeled herself to not look his way. Though presumably they have recently eaten, the jury have none of that full-bellied afternoon drowsiness, instead they are alert, clearly focused on these proceedings. I see empathy and pity on the faces of at least three of the women. Sweetie's body language is defiant, perhaps in response to this. Even the judge appears to be moved by compassion for her. He asks whether she is okay to carry on giving evidence, whether there is anything that would make the process easier, advises she can take a break when she needs to, have water if she wants, sit or stand to give her evidence, whatever is most comfortable, and she thanks him, has a glass of water, takes a seat.

Quigg continues the afternoon session where she left off, with Tyson Manley returning to Sweetie's on the day she was released from the hospital, reiterates that he was dressed in the brown top and jogging bottoms and trainers we've already heard about in evidence from Kwame and Nadine, and seen on the CCTV footage of the killer walking down the high street in the direction of Sweetie's home.

The first thing he did when he arrived was ring one of his friends to get him some new clothes. Then he took off everything he was wearing, including his trainers, put it all into the washing machine, started it up, and ran himself a bath. Sweetie knew exactly what this meant; he was getting rid of forensic evidence. It wasn't the first time she'd seen him do this and she knew better than to ask questions. While she was rinsing shampoo out of his hair in the bath, he told her he'd arrived at hers at four o'clock. Again she knew exactly what this meant; she was to be his alibi for whatever had gone down.

One of his friends brought around the new purchases and took the wet clothing from the washing machine away with him when he left. She refuses to name names, says she's already in enough problems, doesn't need any more, and Quigg doesn't push, just moves the conversation on. Again I remind myself that she is an expert at this, that there must be a reason for her not exploring this.

Her first confirmation that it was Ryan came hours later. Because Tyson was hungry and she didn't feel up to cooking, they had phoned out for a pizza delivery. Tyson was tucking into it and she was sitting on the floor, at his feet, her back leaned against the sofa, rolling a spliff, when the murder was mentioned on the news and Ryan was named. She smoked that spliff and went to bed. Nothing was said by either of them about the killing. Tyson left her home the next morning about eight thirty, and a couple of hours later the police were at her door and she was transported to the station to make her statement.

I have a vision of her being interviewed at the station, beaten and broken, giving the statement she'd been primed to give. The police must have noticed her injuries. Did anyone ask what had happened to her? Did they care? Has anyone truly ever cared about this girl other than my son?

Quigg pushes on with her questioning. She is trying to establish how realistic Sweetie was to be afraid. Quigg wants to know why she did not come clean afterward, once Manley had been remanded in custody and it was impossible for him to harm her, even if he wanted to. Sweetie tells the courtroom that although he was in prison, his friends weren't, that even though Tyson couldn't physically get at her himself, if he wanted to, he just needed to ask his crew.

Quigg asks, "Is that something that happened to you?"

"What?"

"Friends of the defendant doing something to you on his behalf while he was in prison? Can you give the court an example of a circumstance when that happened?"

"Yeah, I can."

"Would you please?"

"One of his friends gave me a VO to go see him . . ."

"A visiting order?"

"Yeah."

"To go and see the defendant in prison?"

"Yeah. I went and he told me he knew Ryan's funeral was gonna be the next week. He must'a found out from his boys, or maybe he heard it on the news, I dunno. Anyway, there wasn't a connection between him and Ryan then. Like he'd got remanded, but there wasn't nothing to link Tyson to Ryan. All the phone records and that, the police never had them yet, so they never knew me and Ryan had been calling each other. Tyson thought if I went to the funeral, the police might be there undercover and if they saw me there, I would be the link, so he told me not to go. I was still thinking about it. I was thinking I could like go and wear a veil or something and no one would even know it was me, but in the end his crew took care of it."

"How exactly did they take care of it?"

"They came to my yard the night before, three of them, and they went through my wardrobe, took every piece'a clothing I had, stuck them in black bags, every last garment, even the clothes I was wearing, knickers, bra, shoes, the lot. All they left was a dressing gown and a pair of socks, so that was the end of it. Like even if I wannid, I couldn't go, 'cause they made sure I never had nothing to wear."

Quigg finishes her questions just after three and the judge suggests we have a short recess before St. Clare begins asking the further questions he has prepared. When we return to the courtroom and St. Clare stands to proceed, the atmosphere inside the courtroom is palpably frosty. From beside me, Lorna whispers, "I don't know if I can watch this." I take hold of her hand.

St. Clare puts his hands into the pockets of his trousers. He's trying to create the impression this is not a fight, just a friendly discussion between himself and his hostile witness. The expression on her face is bare hatred.

"Miss Nelson . . ."

"Yeah?"

"The story you have told today is a rather grim one . . ."

"It ain't no story."

"Of gangsters who have threatened you, commandeered your phone, taken your clothing, forced you to lie under oath."

"And I never said nothing 'bout no 'gangsters.' "

"However, while it is all very tragic to listen to, it's rather more difficult to establish how much of what you have told us is true and how much of it has simply been made up."

Sweetie continues glaring.

"The one thing that has been clearly established, is the extent to which you are prepared to lie in order to get what you want."

"I'm not no liar."

"Shall we have a look at the facts? You have, by your own admission, lied to Ryan Williams."

"I *never* lied to Ryan!"

"In fact, you did, by not telling him of your . . . *attachment*, shall we say, to Mr. Manley."

"Yeah, but I told you the reason for that."

"You've also lied to the defendant, Mr. Manley, about the nature of your relationship with Ryan Williams . . ."

"To protect Ryan. I said what I needed to say to protect him . . ."

"Despite the evidence you have given here today regarding Mr. Manley, had he given permission, you would have willfully put his name on your daughter's birth certificate, knowing full well there was every chance he was not the father of your child at all."

Sweetie does not answer, just glares at St. Clare.

"Even the evidence you have given this court hinges upon us believing you lied when you made your original statement to the police."

"What I said was what I was told to say."

"The fact is you have told a lot of lies to a lot of people at a lot of different times. Would you agree with that statement?"

She's fuming, Sweetie. St. Clare has successfully backed her up into a corner. She would go for it, I think, if we were anywhere other than this courtroom, go for him, but in this space, she is powerless. She is furious because she is going to have to call herself a liar. I am willing her to calm down because St. Clare is not angry in the slightest. He is systematic and relentless. Anger will not be to her advantage. St. Clare addresses the judge.

"My Lord, if it pleases the court, Miss Nelson may be reminded that she is obliged to answer the questions put to her."

The judge says, "Miss Nelson, you are under oath. Please answer the question."

St. Clare says, "Would you agree that you have told a lot of lies?"

"Only when I had to."

"I would like you to answer directly, Miss Nelson, yes or no; have you or have you not told a lot of lies?"

A pause, then she says, "Okay. Whatever; yeah, I have."

"Despite the fact you have told us you were scared of Mr. Manley, you voluntarily visited him in prison, did you not?"

"Yeah."

"You have told us a story which, if it were true, would make him the last person on the planet you'd wish to visit, yet visit is what you did, and more, during that visit, begged him to allow you to put his name on your child's birth certificate."

"I wannid that protection for her . . ."

"Considering the circumstances, can you honestly say you expected Mr. Manley to agree?"

" 'S the only thing I ever asked him for . . ."

"But did you actually *expect* him to give his consent?"

"Yeah, I did. I did expect that."

"So you were surprised when he refused?"

"No, I weren't surprised."

"You weren't? Then how did you feel?"

"How d'you think I felt?"

"I really couldn't say. Frustrated? Disappointed? Let down?"

"No, what I felt weren't some little 'letdown.' "

St. Clare's voice is louder. "Then how *did* you feel?"

"After everything I did for him, the shit I went through . . ."

"After all that, he still said no. How did that make you feel?"

"It was just to spite me, no other reason, just spite . . ."

The words are fired from St. Clare's mouth like bullets. "And how did you feel about that, Miss Nelson? How did it make you feel?"

"You wanna know how I felt? You really wanna know? I tell you how I felt. I wannid to kill him!"

I close my eyes. The courtroom is silent. She has given him the very ammunition he was after to bolster their defense, handed it to them on a plate. St. Clare is deliberately slow, allows everyone sufficient time to absorb her words, for them to properly sink in.

"But you couldn't kill him, could you? Instead, you had to settle for the next best thing, coming to court and lying that the statement you made on the day following the murder of Ryan Williams was not true?"

Sweetie doesn't answer. I wish she would but she doesn't. Instead she glares at St. Clare as if she would like to kill him too.

"My Lord, I have no further questions for this witness," he says.

The judge thanks Sweetie for the evidence she has given. She nods her head in acknowledgment. Her back is rigid, but as she picks up her bag and steps out of the box, the bravado that has sustained her evaporates. Her shoulders become rounded, her movements jerky with nerves, and she keeps her head down as she leaves. It feels like she is exiting one world and entering another, headed back into her real life, where there are no security guards or protection, where, as she said, they know to find her, and the rules of this courtroom no longer apply. I feel sick with fear for her, for that baby, as I watch her go. I failed to keep my son safe, and it feels this moment as though I have failed her as well.

I look over at Tyson Manley. He looks like someone making an unsuccessful effort to not gloat, a person whose delight is impossible to contain. And why should he contain it? He killed my son and he's never going to have to pay. One opportunity, that's all we had, one chance to nail him, just the one trial. If he gets away with this, if he is found not guilty, he walks away from the charge of Ryan's murder forever. From the expression on his face, he's mentally choosing the shoes in which he'll do that walk.

St. Clare goes over to the glass wall and there is a brief whispered discussion between him and his client. Then St. Clare advises the judge that he will be calling Tyson Manley to the stand tomorrow morning as his final witness. I can feel my heart accelerating. Not only is he going to get off, but he's going to have the opportunity to stand in front of us and make a mockery of Ryan's death and this process. I don't think I can face it, don't think I will be able to sit here and listen to his smug denials. As the judge dismisses the jury, Lorna whispers to Nipa across me that we'd like to speak to Quigg. It is a moment before I am able to stand. In the end we are the last people to leave the public gallery, and try as I might, I cannot stop myself from crying as we make our way to the main foyer of the Old Bailey.

8

QUIGG IS UNABLE TO MEET with us in person. Kwame stands with Nipa, and Lorna sits beside me on a bench, an arm around my shoulders as she asks Henry Taylor-Myles what exactly Sweetie's evidence means for this trial. He has a gentle, intelligent voice, and he speaks more quietly than usual in this public space, telling us Sweetie's evidence has done more harm than good.

I say, "What if she wasn't mugged? What if it was Tyson who beat Sweetie up and put her in the hospital?"

"If it was Mr. Manley," he says, "and she had said that on the stand, the case would've been thrown out. We would have had to have a retrial. You can't charge someone with murder then, halfway through the case, begin accusing them of other offenses. It's very difficult to simply submit new information once the trial has started. If Miss Nelson had said Mr. Manley was responsible for her injuries, it would have been highly prejudicial. It would not have helped at all."

But I think maybe it would have helped. At this point, maybe the case being thrown out would have been to our advantage, the opportunity to go away and reassemble with all the information we now know. I can't understand this process, don't understand the concern, the fairness and consideration at every stage of these proceedings for those who have exercised no fairness or consideration in their dealings with others, the notion that to be clear about this defendant's actions the day before my son was killed would be "highly prejudicial"? What does that even mean? That the evidence might lead the jury to convict this person who deserves conviction?

I say, "So that's why Quigg let the mugging go?"

Henry says, "Yes. The moment Miss Nelson brought it up, we knew we were already treading a very fine line."

"What he did to Sweetie should strengthen our case, not go against it," Lorna says.

Henry answers, "Theoretically, I agree with you, but that's not how the process works. If we had known her evidence in advance, if we had wanted to admit it, we would have called the nurse or doctor who treated her to provide details of her injuries. We would have been able to substantiate them. As it stands, we would only have her word for it, and St. Clare has done an effective job establishing she is capable of lying when it suits her." He looks at me. "I'm sorry. I know this is not what you want to hear."

"He's gonna get off, isn't he?" I ask.

"I think much will depend on how Mr. Manley performs on the stand tomorrow," Henry says. "It's difficult to call. Let's wait and see."

"I'm surprised St. Clare even wants him on the stand," Lorna says.

"Well, I happen to know he doesn't," Henry answers. "But

it's not his decision as to whether Mr. Manley takes the stand or not. Barristers give advice and take instruction. The decision to take the stand is Mr. Manley's."

"Why would he *choose* to do that?" Lorna asks.

Kwame responds, "He's showing off. He thinks the case is in the bag and he's showing off."

"Showing off?" Lorna asks.

"Sadly that may be true," Henry says. "The reason these boys end up here in the first place, often the reason they end up going down, it's all about 'show.'"

We leave when Henry does, gather in the passage outside the entrance to the public galleries, and Lorna talks to Nipa about Sweetie. Nipa promises to look into her circumstances and let us know what is being done. I wait beside Kwame while Lorna presses her to look into it this very evening. Nipa assures us she will. Then we depart, Nipa and I to her car, and Lorna and Kwame to the tube station for their journeys home by public transport. The drive is quick and quiet, my head filled with the court day. After Nipa leaves, I loiter outside my home, note there have been a few more bunches of flowers left, adding to the growing shrine on the street beside my garden wall, another teddy, more cards containing messages of remembrance. I take my time looking through these wishes and condolences, needing something to lift me, which they do while simultaneously cutting me down. I leave them where they are and go inside.

I am relieved Lloydie is not in. As usual, he has cooked dinner and the pots are still warm on top of the stove, but I cannot eat. My stomach is a knotted mass of tension, my thoughts so wild, swinging between Lloydie's allotment,

Sweetie's evidence, trying not to think about Tyson Manley and tomorrow, sitting there listening to him deny everything, reducing the truth to the performance that best serves himself and St. Clare and their case. Instead of food I pour a vodka and take it upstairs, run a bath. After undressing and putting on my dressing gown, I go back down and replenish my glass. In the bathroom when I turn off the water and shed my robe, I catch sight of someone in the misted mirror glass, and I start, thinking someone else is in the room before swiping my arm across the moisture, clearing a rippled strip to expose a skinny woman whose rib cage is sharply defined, risen above the hollows in the spaces between, borderline skeletal and virtually bald, and I look away from my refection, offended by it. It is impossible to reconcile her with the image of myself I have in my mind. No wonder Lloydie is no longer interested. How could he be when I can hardly bear to look at myself? I get into the bath, lie back, close my eyes, and think about Sweetie.

There are so many things I supported Ryan with; all that wasted GCSE revision, being organized about his homework, ensuring he had the correct books and kit and equipment, replacing his Oyster card after he lost it, working out how to get him and his friends to ice-skating, without an adult, by public transport, checking out the links to get them there and safely back, the entire route, the timings, no small detail overlooked or issue left to chance; months spent practicing tying his shoelaces, the painstaking process of teaching him to tell the time. Sweetie is seventeen years old, a mother already, has at best been neglected as a child, badly beaten—maybe worse—living in fear in the place she should feel safest, and as far as I can see it has been with zero support, not in Bangladesh or Cape Town but here in the developed world that is the UK, no interest and little kindness from anyone, except that small amount for so short a time given by my son. How does this girl restore her life? Is it possible for that process to happen alongside her being a full-time single mum? I have no idea where you begin in the hope of breaking such a cycle, how to go about effecting change so that in another seventeen years her baby isn't hanging around the wrong boys, being passed around like a serf, taking drugs, maybe pregnant herself. There's so much stacked against her and all of it so vast. If she wanted her daughter to have a different, a better life, where would she begin?

I am disoriented as I sit up with a splash, surprised to discover I fell asleep in the bath, that I must have been asleep for a while, because the water has gone cool. It was a sound that woke me and I listen for it, hear it coming from downstairs, short bursts of frantic tapping, like someone rapping on glass. I get up and out of the bathtub, wrap a towel around myself. I go into the bedroom, look out the window, see no one on the doorstep. I hear the sound again. It's definitely someone knocking. By the time I get downstairs to the front door it has stopped. I shout, "Who is it?"

The tapping begins again but it's coming from the side door that leads directly into the kitchen. I go into the kitchen, look through the window. It's her, Sweetie.

As I open the door she rushes in, closes it fast behind her, looks through the window as though checking for other people, quickly closes the blinds then turns around to face me. The fear on her face escalates the fear I feel as well. She is everything I have avoided, this girl, everything from which I sought to protect my son, from the parts of the city I have consciously held at arm's length, that volatile place where things are not only bleak but relentless, where anarchy reigns and violence is king.

"I got nowhere to go," she says. "The hospital's discharged us. I said I had to go home and get the baby's clothes, but they've been there already, the door's all kicked off, the place's been trashed. They're gonna kill me."

I think about the guy who was with Ms. Manley this morning in court, who did not return after lunch, how ominous it seemed then.

She says, "I can't go back. I shouldn't have come here, but I got nowhere else to go."

"Sweetie, you need to go to the police . . ."

"I ain't going to no police station! What they gonna do? Stick me in some hostel? I know girls who've done that, gone to the police and been put in some hostel. They'll send other girls to the police who'll get put into those same hostels too, and when they find you, you won't even know it. Next thing you're sitting there thinking you're safe and the door's being kicked in!"

"Sweetie, they're the only people who can help you . . ."

"Then there's no one that can help! Oh God . . . What am I gonna do? I gotta get away . . ."

"Calm down—"

"I gave evidence against Tyson! I'm not gonna be the fucking message they send to other people to keep their mouths shut. I gotta leave the country . . ."

"Do you have a passport? Money? Go to what country? How're you gonna live?"

"You're not hearing me! They know where I live!"

"I'm not telling you to go back. I'm saying we need to calm

down . . . think this through. There's always an answer. We just need to find it."

She's wearing the clothes she had on earlier in court, Lorna's cardigan buttoned almost to the top. I have no idea whether she has any money or if she's actually eaten today. "Look, sit down. Let me think about this. You're hungry, aren't you? Let me make you something to eat."

As I dish her up a plate of food and microwave it I ask, "The baby's still at the hospital?"

"Yeah, but I gotta pick her up tonight. They need the bed."

"How is she?" I ask, maybe my grandchild, born into this reality so grim.

"Tiny," she says, "like a dolly of me."

I put the plate down in front of her, some cutlery. "Eat. Let me get dressed. I'll be back in a minute."

She is hungry, dives in. I'm about to leave the kitchen, but I pause, turn around, and ask, "You will be here, won't you, when I come back down?"

Her mouth is full. She nods.

"Good. I won't be long."

I pull on my clothes like a madwoman. Gently, I close the bedroom door, phone Lorna, am relieved when she picks up straightaway.

I whisper, "Sweetie's here, downstairs. The hospital's chucking them both out and her flat's been ransacked. She's got nowhere to go."

"Damn! I knew it. God! I should have made Nipa sort it out there and then. You'll have to take her to the police station . . ."

"She won't go to the police. Apparently she can be tracked down if she goes to them."

"Are you serious?"

"That's what she says."

"The hospital's asking her to leave today? Right now?"

"She says they want the bed."

"What? Where's the bloody social worker? The hospital must have one. Have they not spoken to her?"

"I don't know. She didn't say. She seems to have some trust issues."

"Nipa was supposed to sort this out."

"She obviously hasn't."

I walk over to the window, stand to the side, look out into my garden, onto the street, watch a man walking along the pavement, just some regular guy going about his business, berate myself for the paranoia, step back.

Lorna says, "Call her a cab. Give her my address . . ."

"No."

"They can stay in Leah's room . . ."

"I said no."

"Do you have a better plan?"

"Lorna, we don't know anything about her. All this stuff she's mixed up in, these people, you've got no idea what you might be bringing into your home."

"So what's your advice? Just leave her to sort her problems out herself? Put her out and close the door?"

"I think we should call Nipa."

"If you think she'll agree, you can speak to her about it. If you go behind her back to Nipa, she won't trust us either. Marce, she has a baby . . ."

"I know."

"That could be Ryan's—"

"I know, I *know* that!"

"She needs help."

I don't answer because I know Sweetie won't want me to ring Nipa and she obviously has nowhere to go. And because of that baby.

"She's already freaking me out. She's scared she's being followed. There could be people waiting for her at the hospital, they might follow her from there to yours."

"You're right, don't send her back to the hospital on her own. If you think it's safe, just put her in a cab to mine. I'll ring Kwame, ask him to go with her to get the baby. I think that's a better plan."

"Kwame?"

"Yes, *Kwame.*"

A million missed signs collide; the eye contact between them, a chemistry I wasn't focused on, a meeting of minds. I love her and I trust him. "Okay."

"Write it down for her, the address, in case she forgets it."

"I will."

"Send her to me. I'll be damned if this girl's gonna slip through any more cracks."

At the bottom of the stairs, I pause and press the handle of the front door to check it is properly closed. I put my eye to the spyhole and look through it to outside. The whole thing is ridiculous. I am being ridiculous. Outside looks like outside, like it does all the time. I feel a movement brush past the backs of my legs and nearly jump out of my skin before I realize it is Sheba, and she's hungry, just woken up and ready to be fed. She makes it clear, taking a few steps toward the kitchen, her bowl, stopping and waiting to be followed. I hesitate at the living room door and she carries on padding toward the kitchen. I go into the living room, check the windows are locked while looking outside, checking the street. The street looks like the street. I draw the curtains, then head for the kitchen.

She's standing at the sink, her back to me when I enter, staring at a small framed picture of Ryan, taken at school last year, in full uniform. I think you can tell a lot about a person from a good photograph, and the picture she is looking at is one of my favorites. He looks like Lloydie when I first met him, when we were young, yet there are traces of me, around his eyes, in his smile. He looks so healthy and happy, so healthy and happy and young and full of promise. He was such a handsome boy, his skin tone an even muscovado brown. His cheeks are full, his eyes intelligent and soft; that's what that photo managed to capture so piercingly, his intelligence and his softness, his beautiful interior world that was demonstrated in the way he spoke, the way he cuddled back. Her shoulders are heaving as she sobs. Sweetie turns around.

"I never meant for this to happen. I swear to God, I never meant for none of this."

She looks wretched, distraught. As I move toward her to hold her, she steps back, away from me.

"They were already there that night, when I got home, in a car outside my flat, and they came inside. They were drinking and burning and I knew what was coming and I knew there was nothing I could do to stop it. I was so scared. I kept thinking maybe it'll be enough and they'll just leave Ryan alone, but they wouldn't stop. I swore I'd never see him again, I swore and I never did! I told Tyson we went to the same school, that's the only thing I told him, I never wannid to but they wouldn't stop, and that bastard still broke my nose . . ."

"It's okay, Sweetie, you don't have to explain, I understand—"

"No you don't! You don't understand. They recorded it! On their phones! I was crying and begging them to stop and they filmed it. They were laughing when they were recording and they sent it to me, like I was just some big joke. They've all got it, could be watching it and laughing right now! Oh God! It's my fault. Everything! I'm sorry, so so sorry. If I could go back, change everything, I'd do it, on my baby's life. He was the only good thing I ever had, but I'd give it up, every second if it would bring him back, if I could just bring Ryan back."

I take a step toward her again and this time she doesn't back away, but lets me cuddle her, comfort her, hold her head against my breast inside my arms as she cries it out. There were no muggers. There was violence on that day, and worse, but it was Tyson Manley and his friends who did it. I called Ryan inside and closed the door in her face and she went back to the only place she had, where they were waiting because they knew she had nowhere else to go. She was the catalyst, because she existed and caught my son's first-love eye, but this girl did not shape Tyson Manley. She's not responsible for the person he's become. She wanted to be happy, that's all, and she was entitled, that's what he said; sixteen years of age and Ryan knew that already. Happiness, how small a thing to wish for, so tiny and so catastrophic. She was only a little older than Ryan, this mother who is little more than a child, that's what she feels like in my arms, a young girl. I can forgive this, forgive her, have to, in fact. It's the only pathway that leads to the possibility of me ever forgiving myself.

"It's over now. It's okay."

She pulls away from me. "It's not okay. All those people in court thinking I'm nothing but a liar. No, it's not okay. I should've told them what he did! I should have told everyone what really went down. I wannid to, but I just couldn't, I couldn't do it . . ."

"You made the right decision. If you'd told the court what really happened, they would have had to have a retrial, the case would've ended." She would have relived that terrible night, the beating, the filming of it, the laughter of Tyson Manley and his friends. She would have showed the court the mercilessness of his character, and all it would have achieved was the trial coming to an end, either before or just after St. Clare accused her of lying about that as well.

"You know the truth and now I do as well. It doesn't matter what the court thinks."

"It matters a lot, to me."

"There's no point going around it. Right now, this moment, the thing that matters most is what you're going to do."

I sit her down, tell her the plan, such as it is, and write down Lorna's address on a piece of paper while she goes to the bathroom to wash her face and compose herself. Her handbag is on the kitchen chair, the top unzipped. I move the handle to drop the folded sheet of paper inside it. The handle slips, the bag gapes open, and I am astounded to find myself staring at a gun.

It is on the kitchen table in front of me when she returns, on top of a sheet of kitchen roll meant for wiping spills, drying glasses, a world away from what it's being used for now, a barrier between the surface of the table we eat on and this weapon of death. I look up at her. "Is it loaded?"

She doesn't answer, instead walks quickly over to the table, goes to pick it up, but I grab her hand, stop her. "Are you out of your frigging mind?"

She says, "You don't know shit about my life! You got no idea, none! I'd rather die than go through what I went through before, and I'll kill every last fucking one of them, they ever try anything like that again."

"And what about your baby? What should she do when you're dead or serving fifteen years? What happens to her then? You know you'd probably end up in prison if the police just caught you carrying this . . . *thing* around, even if you didn't use it. This is madness, Sweetie, total madness."

"I'm not you! I can't do what you want me to do! You think the police is gonna be beefing up some big campaign 'cause someone rapes me or stabs me or shoots me? If I'm dead, it might get a little shout-out on the local news. They'll say my mother's doing bird 'cause she's a crackhead and I was Tyson's link. People won't even stop eating dinner. They'll be like, "That explains it; *next?*" If I'm gonna make it, if I'm gonna remain alive, it'll be 'cause I did it, I managed, no one caught me slipping and killed me first!"

And finally it is clear to me, I see it, the war Ms. Manley spoke of, the fight not just to be unhurt and unmolested, to stay alive, but to live. Sweetie's right; what do I know about any of this? I let go of her hand, she picks up the gun, wraps the sheet of kitchen roll around it, and I watch as she swaddles it like a baby, puts it back inside her handbag. All I have ever wanted was to protect my little family, the precious people inside it.

"You cannot take that gun into my sister's house. You'll be safe there. You have to trust me."

"Trust? You wanna talk about trust? I don't trust no one, *no one*, not even myself! There's whole cemeteries out there full up of trusting people."

I close my eyes. She's right. It's what she said before, my son was too trusting, and that's exactly where he is, the cemetery. I say, "Sweetie, in court you said you felt with Ryan like you could make a good choice, not between one shit thing and another, but something different, good. Right now, this moment, you have the chance to make that choice again. You can go to my sister's, stay till we sort you out, find you somewhere safe to live, maybe get into a college with a nursery for the baby, find a job, provide a life for you both that is different to what you have now. I'm begging you, put the gun back down, leave it here, please. It belongs in your old world. You have a choice to stay in that world or move out of it into something new."

I look at her. She looks away, down at the floor. She wants more than the tiny tight corner of the world she's been consigned to. That desire, that hope, is what's brought her here. I push. "Well? What's it gonna be?"

She takes the gun out of her bag, and as she does, the piece of paper with Lorna's address on it is pulled out as well and falls to the floor at her feet. She puts the gun back onto the kitchen table, then bends down and picks up the folded sheet, unfolds it, reads the address. She looks up as I stand, watches as I grab the house phone to call her a minicab. I pause a moment before dialing.

"Well done. You probably just made the best decision you'll ever have to make as a mum."

The cabdriver rings me back on the house phone to let us know he has pulled up outside, and from the moment I put the phone down, Sweetie goes up a gear into hyperdrive. She looks out of the living room windows quickly, checking to see if the coast is clear before heading for the side door. Clutching her handbag tightly, she virtually runs from the door to the cab, and belatedly I run after her, my eyes going up and down the street fearfully, looking for I hardly know what, wishing her fear was less contagious, as paranoid now as she is, berating myself for behaving like a fugitive when I'm not. Her head is down, her shoulders rounded, conspicuously avoiding being seen. She practically yanks the back door open and gets in in one movement, slamming it shut behind her. She says something to the driver and the cab has begun to move almost before I have made it to the curbside. Her departure is so swift, I haven't had a chance even to properly say goodbye. I wait a moment so that if she looks out the back window I can give her a reassuring wave, and from nowhere, two figures hurtle past me, running down the center of the road after the cab as it begins picking up speed. One of them almost catches it, but as he can't maintain that pace, and as the cab pulls farther away, he reaches out in frustration and slams the palm of his hand loudly onto its boot. The cab gets to the top of my road and turns left onto the high street.

And I am still standing there, in shock I think, as they both stop running and watch the cab disappear from sight, then finally turn so they are looking at me. My heart inside my chest pounds wildly. I spin casually, as if I have seen nothing, begin walking back to my home as swiftly as I can without looking as though I am trying to get away. I try not to give the appearance of panicking despite the fact that I am. I know consciously, acutely, that I should not look back, because then they will know that I know they were here for Sweetie and now she's gone, possibly for me, but I can't resist it. When my head swivels around, I discover that not only are they no longer standing watching me from the end of the road, they are both jogging in my direction, and from that moment, the pretense is off, and they both begin charging at full speed toward me. They are wearing hoodies, and because it is dark, it is virtually impossible to make out their faces. Now I understand the terror that made Nadine Forrester trip at the Sports Ground. My focus is on two things and two things only, running with all my might as fast as I can to get back to the house, and not falling over on the way.

And I make it to the side door, manage to get myself through it, into the kitchen, grab the door with both hands and have almost shoved it closed when I feel the push from the other side. I imagine one of them has landed a flying dropkick with all his body weight behind it against the door, because it crashes open with a force that sends me flying across the room, hurls me onto the kitchen table, and my weight tips it over and onto me as I fall to the floor. I hear the clatter of a chair as it comes to a stop in the hallway outside the kitchen doorway. I look around desperately and down, and it's there on the floor beside me, Sweetie's gun. I pick it up and stand like a police officer in a gangster movie, both hands wrapped around the grip, the muzzle of the gun and my arms forming a horizontal V, and the effect is instantaneous; they both stop moving so abruptly you might have thought I'd shouted "Freeze!" But I have used no words. I don't need to. What I have in my hands speaks volumes in the language they understand; I have the power to take their lives. Now I can see their faces, here, in the light of the kitchen, scared, two pairs of wide eyes fixed fast upon the jerky movement of the gun. They are young boys, like my son was, mere kids, and they are fearful because they do not want to die.

I move back a little, swinging the muzzle from one to the next to stop them moving forward and closer. They have gotten over the shock now, had time to think about what they're seeing, what they're really looking at; a middle-aged woman with tufts sprouting here and there from her balding head, whose arms are shaking violently as she subdues them with a gun. I really don't need to ask to know they can hardly believe their eyes.

They say that in the moments before you die your life flashes before your eyes. Since Ryan's death, it is something I have thought about a lot, the fact that most people's lives are relatively long, a flash little more than seconds, deduced that in that moment, it has to be the case your brain must be functioning under duress with maximum efficiency, and even then to play out your whole life, even one as short as Ryan's, would be impossible, so your mind must select them for you, the memories of the most important moments, and give them back to you in that instant with such clarity and detail, it feels as if time has virtually ground to a halt. This feels like such a moment, except instead of memories, time has slowed and my mind is filled with thought. I am thinking that I am holding a gun in my hands, *me*, pointing it at these boys as young as Ryan, and the whole scenario is insane; I am as far removed from taking life as it is possible for a human to be.

This is Sweetie's world, not mine, the world of those who have nothing to lose, people without functioning families or jobs or prospects or hope, and I am not one of those people. The life I have, though broken, still has value to me and I won't spend the next decade of it sitting in an anger management circle with other prisoners, discussing how I came to be at Holloway serving life. I have a choice to make here, like Sweetie, and I need to make it fast before this all goes horribly, horribly wrong, before the moment shifts and one of them moves, and from sheer terror, I fire and one of them ends up dead. I lower my hands to the floor, drop the gun, take a couple of steps back away from it, from them, feel the unyielding coolness of the kitchen wall pressed against my back.

The boy on the left steps forward, picks up the gun, checks the cylinder, says to his accomplice with a laugh, "And there's bullets in it an' all, bro." They both laugh. He clicks the cylinder back into place, presses the cold metal muzzle against my temple hard, and says, "Playtime's over. Where's she gone?"

I don't answer. It's not just my arms, my whole body is violently shaking. I hear a click beside my ear, which at first I think is the sound of the gun firing, then realize I'm still alive, he's merely cocked the hammer; *I'm such a novice.* All those action films I sat through with Ryan, and I still forgot when I was holding the gun that before you can shoot, the hammer needs to be cocked. He presses the gun harder against my head. Now it hurts.

"This is your last chance; where's she gone?"

I say the only words I have in my mind. "If I was your mother, I would've loved you."

The expression on this young boy's face shifts from anger to confusion to sheer astonishment. His accomplice asks him, "Wha'd she fucking say?"

And perhaps because he can think of no appropriate response, the boy in front of me pulls his arm back and swipes me across the head full-force with the gun and the power goes down. The blow stuns me. My legs give way and I feel my body weight hit the floor. My eyes are closed. The pain is intense, and I can feel blood running across my face, warm, sticky, and plentiful. I lie there and wait for him to finish me off. Now is the moment for my life to flash before my eyes, but the life I see is not mine, it's Ryan's; newborn, just lying there, eyes wide and unfocused; as a toddler, eating finger paint, his mouth a cave in the middle of an azure lagoon; running barefoot across the sand, his dragon kite figure-eighting the skies; meticulously wiping the earth from his hands above a newly created mound. I am ready.

Death is a roaring baritone howl that hurtles through a tunnel toward me, so loud and unexpected that I open my eyes, see Lloydie with a kitchen chair in his hands above his head, watch him bring it down with all his might onto the head and arm of the boy holding the gun. The gun discharges with a bang, flips from his grasp, crosses the laminated flooring in a clatter to land in the corner. I hear the disintegration of plaster and glass. The stunned boy collapses to the floor. His accomplice raises his hands defensively as Lloydie takes the chair up again, three-legged now, brings it crashing down onto him in turn. The first boy, behind him on the floor, gets up, leaps onto Lloydie's back, and I watch Lloydie begin to buckle under the weight, stumbling backward frantically till he comes to a hard stop, the boy on his back crushed between Lloydie's weight and the wall behind them both, and as Lloydie turns around and lands a powerful punch to his stomach, the boy falls to the floor in a winded heap clutching his waist, rolls over, moans. Lloydie turns around, begins heading back to the accomplice, on his knees now, disoriented but rising to his feet. As Lloydie reaches for him he takes a step back, a drunken stagger, shakes his head, and maybe clears it, because he turns and bolts, legs it out through the side door and is gone. Lloydie charges after him, gets to the door, stops, looks out, looks to me, then his gaze comes to rest on the boy still on the floor.

The boy's response is panicked. He tries to shuffle backward, away, but there is nowhere to go, nothing behind him but wall. Lloydie grabs him by the back of his top, hauls him to his feet with one hand, uses the other to pin him fast against the wall with a hand gripped hard around his throat. The boy's words are a choked gasp. "I was just gonna scare her, I swear to God!"

And he is transformed in an instant, not a member of an organized criminal fraternity, not some sophisticated mercenary or old-style East End hard nut, just a young boy, eyes bulging wide, looking exactly like what he is; a terrified kid.

Lloydie pulls his arm back for the punch, and I see in his expression that this man, whose strong hands have never hurt a living soul, has inside him this moment the capacity to kill. "You like scaring women, do you? Try me! Go on, scare me!"

I hear my voice shouting, "Lloydie, no!" I don't know how I've gotten up or crossed the floor, but I am behind him, my hands locked around his elbow, pulling it back, crying, shouting, "Stop, please stop!"

He is much stronger than I am and as he jerks his arm back hard, I lose my grip and stagger backward, falling clumsily across the kitchen sink unit, hear the contents of the dish rack falling, spilling, breaking, bang my hip hard against the edge of the countertop, cry out in pain. Lloydie turns, and I see in his eyes that he finally *sees* me. He releases the boy's throat, runs over, lifts me from the floor. The boy behind him collapses to his knees for a second only, spots his chance, and takes it. He is out through the side door in a flash. Lloydie lets me go, runs after him, gives chase. I hurry to the side door also, praying he doesn't catch him, that the person who ends up sitting in the anger management circle in prison doesn't turn out to be my husband. I am relieved to see he has stopped at the gatepost, glaring in frustration down the street, presumably watching that young boy flee. Abruptly he turns around, walks back fast, passes me, is in the kitchen again.

"They've gone," he says, pushing the door closed behind him, discovering it no longer remains closed, wedging another of the chairs beneath the handle to make it secure. "Are you okay?"

"I'm fine," I say, touching my head, and it's true. "I'm okay."

He picks up the landline, begins to dial.

"What are you doing?" I ask.

"Calling the police. They brought a gun into our home! A gun!"

I take the phone from him. "Stop. Wait."

"For what?"

"I can't think."

"He's getting away!"

"They didn't bring it. The gun was already here."

"*What?*"

"I'll tell you everything in a moment, Lloydie, but right now I have to call my sister."

Though I play down what has just happened, on the phone to Lorna, I have to tell her so she is not caught off guard as I was. Neither Kwame nor Sweetie has arrived at her home yet, and she tells me not to worry about her, that they will be vigilant and she'll call me back later once the baby's been picked

up. Then I have to reassure her that Lloydie and I are okay. I
don't tell her about the gash on my head that I'm pressing a
clean tea towel against as we speak. Lloydie tidies up, rights
the table, begins to sweep up smashed crockery and glass. He
stops to pick up the gun with a screwdriver through the trig-
ger hole, like a police officer concerned about contamination
of evidence, looks around wondering where exactly to put it,
pulls out a freezer bag, drops it inside, and places the bag on
top of the fridge. He is impatient, waiting for me to get off
the phone to explain to him what on earth's going on. When
I put the phone down, I do.

I tell him about my meeting with Sweetie and her evidence, sitting on a chair as he cleans the blood from my scalp
and face. There is a gash above my ear, bruising around it,
but crucially, no splintered bone or gray matter. As he dresses
it, I tell him about the baby, and he has to sit down. I present
the information to him stressing how unlikely it is that she's
Ryan's, in order not to get his hopes up unnecessarily, but
the effect it has on Lloydie is the effect it had on me. He can
hardly believe the possibility exists, the chance, however minute it may be. He has to get the calendar down from the wall,
work out when Ryan died, when she came here for that first
visit, count the weeks forward ending two weeks ago.

And then he can't talk about it anymore, as if the mere
speaking of it, the airing of his wish, the statement of his
hope, might be enough to jinx it, so I tell him about Sweetie's
visit earlier, leading up to the moment he arrived back home.
That brings our discussion back to our starting point, and
the fact that Lloydie still thinks we should call the police.

"But if we go to them, we're gonna have to lie," I say.
"There's no way we can tell them that gun was already here.

Where're we gonna say it came from? We can't say Sweetie brought it."

"We'll leave her out of it. Why can't we just say you were attacked?"

"And supposing the police actually catch those boys? What if they come clean and tell the truth? What if they deny it? Are we going to go to trial and get up in court and lie? That's perjury, Lloydie. Are you prepared to do that?"

"If we do nothing, then they just get away with it," Lloydie says, and I remember my discussion with Sweetie at Hulya's, where from the privilege of my position outside her world, I told her pretty much the same thing.

"They haven't gotten away with it," I say. "You beat them up. Way the law works, for all I know, they can probably do you for assault. My biggest worry is if they come back."

"Back? Here? I hope they do so I can finish the job!"

My head aches. I take a couple of paracetamol, and some cranberry without the vodka, go into the living room, and lie down while Lloydie gets his toolbox out and begins to repair the hinge side of the door frame, listen to the whir of his electric tools as he secures our home. I wake up when the phone rings. It is Lorna. Kwame and Sweetie are back safely from the hospital with the baby. They don't think anyone was waiting or followed them.

"So everyone's okay, then?"

"Yes," Lorna says. "You should see this baby, Marce; she's so diddy and gorgeous."

After speaking to her I get up, go into the kitchen, where Lloydie is repairing the chair he virtually smashed to pieces on those boys. He looks up, meets my eye, connects. Chaos and disorder and confusion, threats and violence and damage, and here we are on the other side of it, and while it may be too early to hope for the long term, for now, this moment, my husband is back.

"They're all at Lorna's. Everyone's fine," I say. "I'm going upstairs to lie down, unless you need me to do something . . ."

"You go. I'm just gonna finish up down here, then I'll be up." I say, "Okay."

I turn the bedroom light on then off when I enter the room, go over to the window, stand back a little from the net curtains, and look out into the street. It looks like the street. Quiet. Calm. Unthreatening. It is unbelievable, everything that has happened in this one evening. I change into my nightwear and lie on the bed.

I am asleep when Lloydie gets onto the bed beside me, feel him adjusting the covers, pulling them up to cover me, getting under them himself. I have my back to him and he adjusts himself so that his front is pressed against my back. His arm goes around my waist and I take the palm of his hand in mine, hold it. It is enough.

The next time I awaken, though it is still dark outside, I hear birdsong. Lloydie's desire is a hot pulse wedged against the base of my spine. He trails a hand gently over the side of my body from hip to waist, then again. I turn over to face him, can see in the dark room his opened eyes, put my arms around him, and hold him. He kisses me. It is not a chaste kiss, nor is it the experienced kiss of a man married for eighteen years who has kissed his wife a thousand times; it is a request, a gentle kiss that seeks permission.

It is strange, our consummation, like a blues composition put together by two individuals with differing styles. I am desperate for this connection, pull hard at his pajama top, impatient to remove it, feel buttons pop. And he is the opposite, slow, meticulously careful to cause no harm through haste, no accidental hurt in a moment driven more by need than thought. His undressing of this new body of mine is slow. His mouth follows his hands, exploring each part as it is exposed, not just those bits directly connected with the act, but everywhere, my scarecrow's neck, the deeply hollowed blades of my shoulders, grazes the insides of my elbow with the tip of his tongue, uses it to measure the crazy pulse racing below the parchment-thin skin. He is intent on rediscovering every nook of this body that has been through so much, changed so much, which has been untouched for too long, and this voyage for him is a voyage for me, I who thought the part inside me capable of feeling passion might have been taken from me forever alongside my boy.

When it comes, the release from this agony of feeling is violent, all-consuming, a million shattered pieces brought together in an implosion that leaves me shocked and my husband lying on top of me sobbing, shaking like an addict marooned from his drugs, or maybe an addict who was marooned and has just discovered a life raft. I hold on to him fiercely, say over and over, "It's okay, Lloydie, it's okay," and I think perhaps it may be. What we have done was not so much making love but making life in the After. I hope that if Ryan is out there somewhere, if he can see us both right now, he would not only understand; he'd be happy.

9

THERE IS A CUP OF tea on the side when I awaken. Lloy-die is not in the room, neither is Sheba. I ring Lorna while I drink the tea. I want to tell her about our enormous transi-tion, but it feels like something a teenager would do and too complex to talk about just yet, immature and premature. But she hears something in my voice anyway because she asks, "What's going on with you?"

I laugh. "Mind your own business. I'm just checking you guys are okay."

She tells me they're all okay. Sweetie and her daughter are both sleeping. It was nearly ten by the time they got to hers last night, and the baby didn't settle down till after midnight. She takes a bottle, so Lorna fed her this morning around five. She says, "Kwame stayed over."

"Really?" I say.

She can hear raised eyebrows in my tone, I think, because she adds, "On the sofa."

"You don't need to explain anything to me . . ."

"He's staying today as well, with the two of them, while I'm at court, just to be on the safe side."

I say, "That's good." I have finished drinking my tea. "Really, it is."

After I have my shower and return to the bedroom, Lloydie is sitting on his side of the bed, dressed in suit pants and shirt and tie, buffing his shoes. He smiles at me. I smile back.

Nipa manages to perfectly conceal her surprise when I get to the car with Lloydie. A passerby might have thought we were in the middle of a weekday routine, us three. He gets into the backseat and I get into the passenger seat beside her. We make small talk on the journey there as if the three of us have been making small talk every day of the last week. But there is a moment at a set of traffic lights, while we are waiting for them to change, when it is silent and she gives me a sidelong glance and a smile that says "Bloody marvelous." I give her one back. It is.

Almost as soon as we take our seats in the public gallery, a waft of fragrance as intense as the inside of a perfumery announces Ms. Manley's arrival, on time again for the second day in a row. After years of ticking idly, her alarm clock must be in a state of shock. She has with her the young guy who was here on Monday and an even younger boy, maybe fourteen or fifteen years old, who looks so much like Tyson Manley, he has to be the brother, her youngest son. They crowd into their end of the front row and we are seated at ours; Lloydie in the seat Lorna has been occupying, me sitting beside him, Lorna next to me, and Nipa on the other side of her, creating the human barrier between us and them. The seats behind us are filled also, with Ricardo and Luke sitting amongst a group of other young people I recognize as friends of Ryan's from school, and the elderly theater couple eagerly anticipating their grand finale. As Tyson Manley enters the witness box, the younger brother watches with the excitement of a child who has gone to watch his elder sibling on the stage. He is smiling. Tyson notices and looks up at him, gives him the nod of acknowledgment customarily reserved for his mother, and the younger brother looks at his mother as if to say "He's seen me. Did you see that nod? He knows I'm here."

It is Friday morning. Term time. Unless there has been a teachers' strike, that boy should be in class. I can't even begin to imagine how the conversation went. Had he been asking all along to come? Had he been harassing her from the beginning to attend court so he could watch his brother's murder trial? Did she weigh the pros and cons of keeping him off, apply the argument of parents who take their children on family holidays during term time, decide education comes in various forms, that he'd learn more being in this courtroom today than behind his classroom desk following the national curriculum?

"I bet he's not in school either," Lorna whispers. "The apple doesn't roll far from the tree."

I just don't understand it. "Collateral damage" is what she said to me, my son was collateral damage in the war that's raging outside. But this war she speaks of, does she question her role in it? If Tyson Manley had gone back to her home instead of Sweetie's, would she have put his stuff into the washing machine for him, added double portions of stain remover, ensured she put the wash on a high enough temperature to get rid of the forensic evidence, every last trace?

Is this her youngest son's tutorial in How to Take the Stand, prepping for the future, so he'll know what to do when his turn comes? Maybe later they'll analyze Tyson Manley's performance, dissect it over a spliff and a glass of brandy and Babycham, work out which parts of his testimony worked to greatest effect, where he went wrong. What kind of mother is she? This is not the thinking of a woman in her right mind. She's right, there is a war going on outside, but she is not a victim of it, she is a misguided general preparing her troops to charge into it, to die.

"Poor boy," Lorna whispers. "Poor, poor child."

That poor boy's only surviving elder brother stands in the dock now, being sworn in, hand on Bible, swearing to tell the truth, the whole truth, and nothing but the truth, so help him God. He is wearing another suit today, black, befitting the solemnity of the occasion, with a pastel shirt beneath it and probably the least flamboyant tie he owns. I wonder if St. Clare spoke to Ms. Manley about her son's attire, whether he showed her photographs side by side of a courtroom and a VIP room at Stringfellows, explained to her that at each, a different type of smart dress is appropriate.

Tyson Manley seems less comfortable today standing in the witness box, though it can't be for lack of experience. If it was based on his courtroom experience alone, he should be as comfortable as the custody nurse practitioner. It's not being on the stand that makes him feel uncomfortable, I think it is the suit itself; it's not the kind he would have chosen to wear. He stands in the box and, once he's finished swearing the oath, jams his hands into the front pockets of his jacket just as he would have jammed his hands into the pockets of a sweat top he was wearing, pulling the sides and

front into messy bunched tucks, and I get again that juxtaposition of boyishness and manhood that so forcefully struck
me in court on the first day of this trial, the same as the trans-
formation of the boy in my kitchen. He has lied, raped, and
murdered, yet there is no getting around the fact that he is
still a child. I am a citizen of the wealthy first world society
in which this boy has been allowed to grow up with no moral
compass. What is being done to help people like him, people
like that young boy Ms. Manley has deemed it appropriate
to drag along to observe these proceedings today? A hand
in my lap feels for and takes mine. I look down expecting it
to be Lorna's, but it's Lloydie's. I look at him. There are fine
beads of sweat across his forehead despite the coolness of this
space. His expression is ghastly. I squeeze his hand, give him
what I hope passes for a reassuring smile.

St. Clare appears more confident this morning than when
last we saw him. His questions are easy enough for Tyson Manley to answer and designed to give us a sympathetic picture of
his life and background. The court hears that he has recently
turned seventeen, having had his last birthday a month ago
behind bars while on remand. We learn he grew up with his
mother and two brothers, Vito and De-Niro, that he last saw
his father when he was eight years old and has had no contact
with him since, that Vito's father is dead and De-Niro's is currently serving time.

He is polite, says "sir" at the end of some of his responses.
His voice is quiet. He meets St. Clare's eyes with every answer.
If I hadn't been here listening to the evidence over the last
week, if I did not know who he was or what he'd done, if I had
simply met him on the street and had a short interchange
with him, I would probably have thought he was a nice boy,

and if it had happened in the last seven months, that thought would have been followed with *lucky mum*. I think I expected his voice to roar through the courtroom, that the capacity inside a person that permits them to rape and maim and kill would be evident in his mannerisms, the way he spoke. I expected the walls to shake, the stand to spontaneously combust, expected his speaking to have the impact on the room around him that his actions have had on our lives. Instead I am listening as he quietly, politely explains that he thinks Vito was the most affected by his dad not being around when they were growing up, that he was the one who kept getting into trouble with the police, the one his mother could not control. His own life was apparently sitting neatly on the right tracks till Vito was shot and killed in front of him in the park near their home, the killer never brought to justice by the police. He talks about his brother's murder as calmly as if he were describing a scene from a play. I look over at De-Niro. His elbows are on his knees, his palms cup his chin as he leans forward. He looks sad. Interested but sad. His mother, on the other side of him, her eyes concealed behind her large sunglasses, sits ramrod straight in her seat, and presumably she is an expert at concealing her feelings, because she appears entirely unmoved.

"You began getting into trouble after the death of your brother, did you not?"

"Yes, sir."

"Within four months, you had been permanently excluded from school."

"Yes, sir."

"And were you able to start attending a new school straightaway?"

"No."

"Precisely how long were you out of school?"

"Musta been six months."

"And how was that time spent?"

"Hanging 'round. Playing Wii."

"How would you describe that period in your life?"

"I was bored outta my box. Only things I could do cost dosh I never had."

"And it was around this time that you were arrested for the first time?"

"Yeah."

"And what was that for?"

"Possession of marijuana, sir."

"You were convicted for this, I believe?"

"Yeah."

"Would you like to tell us about that conviction?"

He's relaxed, I think, in control. After a pause he says, "The police are always down my estate, always stopping and searching us when we ain't doing nothing or causing no trouble. They say they stop and search the black youth 'cause we're the ones committing the most crime, but at the end of the day ain't it gonna look like we're committing the most crime if it's only our houses being searched, only us being frisked, only our underpants they're looking down? I had a little draw on me, next thing they're saying I'm some big weed dealer, which I weren't. Couldn't convict me for that 'cause they never had the evidence, but they still convicted me for possession. You know how many people get a caution for smoking a spliff? But I got a conviction."

Lorna leans over, whispers, "I really hope his defense isn't gonna be that he was framed by the police 'cause he's black."

I'm hoping in fact it is, a silly defense easily seen through by the jurors. Yet I think about what he says, try to imagine Ryan out of school for half a year, hanging around all day on the streets, wonder what he, the best of boys, would have gotten up to. The point of the compulsory education system we have is that it creates order. Whether each child comes out at the end of it with a barrowful of qualifications is another matter, but it promotes structure and discipline. It does actually usefully occupy young people. It provides the reason to set the alarm and get out of bed, put your uniform on, show up and focus to some extent on the day. What do you do in the absence of that structure, outside the rules, outside society? Was he expected to sit at home educating himself online? One day with nothing to do would have had Ryan climbing the walls; *six months?*

St. Clare has him talking about his mother, how hard she struggled to bring up the three boys on her own, bouts of homelessness, debt, and depression, how difficult it was for her coping with Vito's death. He says it is only recently she has begun to function again, and I hear the subtext loudly; this is a poor guy from a messed-up family, whose mother already has a lot on her plate, and sending this son down, the next one in chronological order still alive, will probably push her over the edge. I think about Ms. Manley, about that single occasion in the toilet, the two of us alone. I know exactly how it feels to have a son killed; of course she's traumatized, of course it took time to get back to a place where it was possible to function, but I look over at her all dolled up in her designer gear, reeking of perfume, half her face concealed by those ridiculous sunglasses, the little skin you can see made up to the nines, and I see nothing that speaks of softness or fragility or sadness. I see instead a woman with something skewed in her value system, something wrong with her priorities. If our circumstances were reversed, I could never have said the horrible words she said to me.

But then I can't determine the extent to which I have the right to judge her, and not just to judge, but to judge on my terms, in comparison with the life I've led. I've never had to bring up three boys on my own. I had one son, who had two parents, and raising him was still a hard task. My mother worked hard to provide, and Lloydie and I have worked hard to provide. We've never been loaded, never not had to concern ourselves with how much money we had coming in, but we have never been destitute, never been without a place to live or been dependent on the system to house and clothe and feed us. Lorna has been a single mother for most of Leah's life, she has done a grand job raising my wonderful niece, and she has done most of it singlehandedly, worked and grafted and raised her child to understand right from wrong, but she has never been without a solid support network. Did Ms. Manley ever have anyone to lean on, to help when she needed it most, someone to take the kids off her hands, occasional respite? And what difference does any of this make anyway? Am I suggesting she is blameless insofar as Ryan's death is concerned, that shitty life circumstances are a form of absolution? Because that's rubbish. Calling my son "collateral damage" wasn't the act of a person who is traumatized, it is the ignorance of a woman who does not know herself what's right or wrong.

St. Clare asks, "Mr. Manley, what are your ambitions?"

"My what?"

"Dreams. For yourself. What do you hope for yourself, for your future?"

It is the first question to which Tyson Manley doesn't have an off-the-cuff response, that he appears to really think about. The pause before he speaks is so long, I begin to wonder if he understands the question. Finally he answers, "I don't have no dreams."

"You must have one."

"Nah, I don't."

"Not one single hope?"

A pause, then, "To be alive still, when I'm older."

My eyes fill. The ache inside me makes my heart pound and that pounding continues throughout the time St. Clare flicks through his papers with slow deliberation, allowing his client's words sufficient time to sink in.

"Mr. Manley, how would you describe the relationship you had with Miss Nelson?"

"She weren't my girlfriend, I'll tell you that much. She hung around the guys and she would sleep with anyone. Yeah, I slept with her from time to time, she was chucking it about like it weren't no big thing. Then she started telling me she wannid us to be girlfriend and boyfriend, like man's gonna wanna be serious about any girl who ain't got no pride in herself."

"So you were not boyfriend and girlfriend?"

"No, sir."

"I see. Much has been made of the fact that Miss Nelson and Ryan Williams, the deceased, were seeing each other and in telephone contact in the months before Mr. Williams was killed. The suggestion is that you were jealous of this relationship and because of this, intended harm to Ryan Williams."

"That ain't true."

"Did you know Ryan Williams?"

"No."

"Have you ever met him?"

"No, sir."

"Are you aware of anyone Miss Nelson has been out with in the past?"

"Seriously, I don't know, but she's slept with near 'nough every man I know."

"And how did you feel about that, knowing that she was seeing other men, 'sleeping' with them, as you say?"

"I never felt no way. She weren't my girl. I couldn't care less."

This is what happens when there are no rules, when there is no adult steering and guiding, when children are allowed to make bad decisions then follow them through. Ms. Manley is responsible for that. How can any woman raise a son so unconscious of any responsibility to treat women with respect, capable of the things this boy has done, able to come into court and lie his head off regarding his actions? What kind of person would keep her youngest son off school to witness this? What on earth does she think he's learning? If my Ryan had ever spoken in my hearing about any girl he'd had relations with in that way, I would have gone in hard. First of all I would have wanted to know if she was so low, what it said about him that he still chose to have intercourse with her? That would have been the starting point and the conversation would have been downhill from there.

"Mr. Manley, as you are doubtless aware, Miss Nelson has made a series of grievous allegations against you. She has said that you and your friends monitored her phone . . ."

"Nah. That ain't true."

"That you listened to a message Ryan Williams left on her telephone and you flew into a rage . . ."

"There woulda had to be some kinda relationship in the first place. I never said she couldn't see who she wannid."

"She says you made threats about 'sorting' her and Ryan Williams . . ."

"That's just lies, man."

"You're saying the evidence Miss Nelson gave to this court yesterday was not true?"

"I'm saying it was bare lies. Bare lies." He shakes his head as if it completely disgusts him; dishonesty disgusts him. A number of the jurors have the same expression on their faces and I wonder if they are merely reflecting his expression or whether, like me, they think he has overplayed his hand, gone just a little too far with the drama. Kwame was right; he is showing off.

St. Clare questions him about Sweetie wanting him to be her baby's official father on the birth certificate, his refusal, the manner in which she stormed off following the discussion, and how this led to Tyson Manley thinking she was going to try to do something to get him back. This neatly brings him back to the issue of why he thinks she lied under oath. They finish up with his version of the events of March 18, his arrival at Sweetie's at four in the afternoon, just as she said in her original statement, more than two hours before the murder occurred, and his assertion that he remained at Sweetie's home till after eight the following morning. By the time St. Clare has finished with his questions, it is quarter to one and the judge directs the court to break for lunch.

Lorna, Lloydie, and I go to the pub over the lunch break. We are a little earlier today than the last time we were here, and it is easier to find a table, quicker to get settled, order.

I say, "I wanted him to explain it to me, that's what I was hoping for, even if I disagreed with his actions, that boy would explain them and maybe I would understand."

"Understand how one kid kills another for nothing? You think there's a way he could've explained it that you would understand?" Lorna asks. "You think he understands? You're probably giving him more credit than he's entitled to. He's had a shitty innings, and he was just jealous."

"No, I don't think you're right. Sweetie said he never cared about her. He doesn't. He doesn't care about anyone. He wasn't some jealous lover . . ."

"He wasn't jealous of Ryan's brains or looks, he was jealous Sweetie had found a route to possibilities, to maybe being happy, when he hasn't, possibly never will. His future's so bleak. He was jealous that for a second it looked like hers might not be."

Lloydie says quietly, "What I don't understand is he looks so . . . *normal.*"

Lorna leans over and gives Lloydie a big hug, rubs his back. Under the table, I take Lloydie's hand. I know exactly what he means. I came to court to hate him. I came to court to see evil personified, and instead of a devil, have found myself looking at a boy, a confused and severely damaged boy the same age as our son.

He says, "I just don't understand it."

I say, "There's no logic, Lloyd, to any of this."

Lorna says, "Marcia's right, there's nothing to understand. It just is."

"What's she like?" I ask. "The baby?"

Lorna smiles. "Gorgeous. She has a tiny curly coolie afro. She's absolutely adorable. I have to stop on the way back and pick them up some bits. When they turned up yesterday, Sweetie had the baby in one arm and a carrier bag on the other, one of those big hospital property bags with all their stuff inside. Everything she has was in her arms. I could have cried."

I remember taking Ryan home the day after he was born. Lloydie had decorated the nursery while I was pregnant. We'd done the shopping for the cot and buggy and car seat. We'd bought a chest of drawers, the one still inside his room now, and the top drawers were filled with delicious tiny baby clothes, the essentials, Babygros and vests and socks and mittens, and gorgeous gift outfits bought by Dan and Rose, friends at work, my mother, Lorna in excited-auntie overdrive. We spent ages trying to decide which outfit we would put on him for his first-ever trip, from hospital to home, couldn't make a decision, brought two in the end to the hospital with us, made the choice of what to dress him in on the day. Lloydie had left us a few hours after Ryan was born, was gone for ages. When we arrived back, dinner had been cooked and there was a bottle of Champagne on the kitchen table, two new flutes beside it. I remember looking at those flutes, at my husband, at the beautiful baby we had made, thinking, *I will never forget this moment, it is perfect.*

"Who does she look like?"

I meant the question to sound more neutral. I should have asked, *Does she look like her mum?* But that's not what I want to ask. I want to ask, Does she look like Ryan? Does she look like Ryan did at the same age?

"She looks like a newborn baby, a tiny sweet newborn baby girl."

"Are they both okay?" Lloydie asks.

"They're fine. They're well. I fed the baby this morning before I left home. Sweetie was sleeping, poor thing. She's exhausted." She shakes her head. "I was watching her while I was feeding the baby and I just couldn't believe someone so young has been through so much."

She could be speaking about Leah, I hear it in her voice, a maternal defense rising; she's ready to fight for her, this girl from the streets, a nobody. I hope Sweetie doesn't let my sister down, that she hasn't robbed Lorna and vacated her flat by the time she gets home. It is an uncharitable thought. Despite St. Clare's efforts to paint her as a compulsive liar, in all my dealings with her, she's been nothing but candid. Our help could do it, help her change her life, completely change the outcome for that baby.

I ask, "Do you think she'd agree to do a DNA test?"

Lorna stops raising her glass to her lips, midway. "Why should she?"

"So we can know for sure, either way, for definite . . ."

"I don't know. I'm not gonna ask her. I don't think you should, either."

"What, you don't think it's important to know whether she's my grandchild or not?"

"No, I don't."

"Well, that's fine for *you* to say." I don't expand, don't add that her child is still living, that hers is the comfortable perspective of those whose children have not been slain, wiped out for good. I don't need to expand, because she knows exactly what I mean and is furious.

"Don't you ever, ever talk to me like I never loved Ryan!

Don't you ever, ever speak to me as if I don't hurt, as if I don't mourn and bleed and cry for him, as if when he died, part of me didn't die with him as well."

"So can't you understand that I *need* to know?"

"Why? Because if that baby is Ryan's child that makes her valuable? Because then, she can count on our support and help and some chance of a decent future? And if she's not, we can all just turn our backs and leave them to fend for themselves? If she doesn't bear your precious genes, Ryan's DNA, it'll be fine for the whole bloody world to ignore her, for her to be chucked out of school, chucked out of society, chucked on the heap, to be drugged up, beaten up, for videos of her being raped to be plastered on YouTube? Don't you understand that's exactly what's wrong with everything?"

"I have a right to know."

"If it's your right, *you* ask."

"It is and I will," I say.

Because I know she is. She has to be my son's child, because I need her to be so much. Because there is nothing more I want, nothing more. It is the only outcome that can bring some sense to the senselessness of what has happened, give us a reason to go on. This baby is my grandchild. Despite the National Lottery odds, someone still wins the jackpot.

Lloydie doesn't look at me as he says, "Supposing she's not?" His voice is quiet, as empty as a cocoa canvas strip.

What if she's not? Suddenly the volume of the noise inside the pub is turned up; people talking, laughing, a woman shouts, the clink of cutlery against plates, a tray of glasses being set down on the side, everything except answers.

Finally Lloydie clears his throat. "So this afternoon's our side's turn to question Manley?" he asks.

Lorna says gently, "Yes."

And the topic is moved to grounds less fraught. We speak only about the case during the rest of our lunch and it strikes me as ironic. Who would have guessed that talking about Ryan's murder trial could ever have been an easement?

Quigg rises to her feet, approaches the witness box boldly, stops in front of it, and smiles at Tyson Manley. He smiles back. It seems a little too much, the smile he gives back, almost a sneer. He doesn't want to smile at all, but he doesn't want to create that impression. He should be concentrating on just giving his evidence but he's not, he's concentrating instead on how he looks. Silly boy.

She thanks Tyson Manley for the evidence he has given to the courtroom and asks if he would mind her asking a few more questions.

He says, "Be my guest."

"Mr. Manley, you have stated under oath that you arrived at Miss Nelson's home on March 18, the day Ryan Williams was killed, at four p.m."

"Yes, ma'am."

"Did you have a key to let yourself in, or did you knock?"

"I knocked."

"And Miss Nelson opened the front door to you?"

"Yes, ma'am."

"So that would have been the first moment you noticed her injuries?"

"I don't know nothing 'bout no injuries."

"I'm asking whether when Miss Nelson opened the front door, you noticed that she had any injuries?"

"And I've told you I don't know nothing 'bout no injuries."

"Mr. Manley, I want to know, after you knocked on the front door, and Miss Nelson opened it and was standing in front of you, did you or did you not notice that she had some injuries?"

"Yeah, I did notice she had some injuries, I'm saying I don't know how she got them."

"So you noticed she had some injuries. You didn't know how they had been sustained. Did you ask her?"

"She said she got mugged."

"Did she tell you she had been hospitalized the previous night and discharged that morning?"

"Yeah."

"Did she tell you what her injuries were?"

"Nah, she never."

"Would you describe for the court the injuries you were able to see for yourself?"

"Er, she had a black eye. And I think her wrist was sprained."

"Was it bandaged?"

"Yeah."

"What about her nose?"

"What about it?"

"Had her nose been broken?"

St. Clare stands. "My Lord, Mr. Manley is neither an orthopedic specialist nor a trauma consultant. He cannot be expected to diagnose any injuries Miss Nelson was unfortunate enough to have sustained."

Quigg says, "I am not asking for a medical opinion, My Lord, merely asking Mr. Manley about any injuries he was able to see when he arrived at Miss Nelson's home and she opened the door to him."

The judge says to St. Clare, "It is, as well you know, perfectly permissible for the witness to be asked what he saw with his own eyes."

"Of course, My Lord. My primary concern is merely that it be clear to the court that while Mr. Manley is able to say what he saw, the actual diagnosis of those injuries is not within his professional expertise, nor to be relied upon as facts in this case."

Quigg says, "I am happy for the jury to be directed as to the fact Mr. Manley is providing a personal opinion only, not medical evidence, in respect of any injuries."

The judge makes some notes, then directs the jury to treat Tyson Manley's evidence as the equivalent of an opinion, not fact, in respect of Sweetie's injuries, as if they, looking at this seventeen-year-old standing awkwardly before them in a grown-up's suit, might mistakenly be under the impression he is an expert medical professional.

Quigg continues. "Thank you, My Lord. Mr. Manley, wholly from the perspective of what you could see with your own eyes in front of you, would you say Miss Nelson's nose had been broken and subsequently treated and dressed?"

He answers, "She had some kinda dressing on it. I ain't no doctor. I can't say if it was broke or what."

"Thank you. Did you ask any questions about her injuries?"

"Nope."

"You have said both in your statement to the police and in evidence here in this courtroom that you arrived at Miss Nelson's home at about four p.m., and that you spent the evening with her watching TV and having sex?"

"Yes."

"That you were so much more interested in having sex than watching the television that you are unable to remember what you watched that evening?"

"Yeah."

"This was the evening of the day on which Miss Nelson had been discharged from the hospital?"

"Yeah."

"Can you recall the time you both went to bed that evening? To sleep?"

"Musta been about ten."

"So you were both having intercourse from about four till ten, when you went to bed?"

"Yeah."

"Six hours?"

"Well, I mean, obviously we stopped a coupla times, had pizza and that."

"So other than a couple of breaks, you were having intercourse for the duration?"

"Yeah."

"Did Miss Nelson appear to be in any discomfort or pain?"

"Nope."

"Did she at any time ask you to stop?"

"If anything, it was the opposite."

"Did that surprise you?"

"Why would it?"

"With her injuries, with her only having been discharged from the hospital the same day, were you surprised she wanted sex, so much of it for so long?"

"I never really thought about it."

"Well, think about it now. Think about those injuries you were able to see for yourself on Miss Nelson when you arrived, a black eye, possibly a sprained wrist, and a broken nose. In retrospect, does it seem likely she would have been in considerable pain and discomfort?"

"Thinking about it now, yeah, I suppose it does."

"Yet you would have us believe that from when you arrived at four till you both fell asleep at about ten, for those six hours, despite the condition she was in, you were both having intercourse?"

"Yeah, we were."

"I see. Mr. Manley, I would like you to read aloud a fragment of the statement you made to the police on March 19, following your arrest. This is a copy of that statement." She hands a bundle of stapled papers to him, folded open. He looks down at it, doesn't look up again. I remember something I read in amongst the pretrial paperwork forwarded to me by Isabelle Rhodes, our solicitor, am surprised someone as competent as Quigg missed it. She continues. "Mr. Manley, would you please read aloud the first sentence of the second paragraph, which begins four lines down the page?"

There is silence. Tyson Manley has not looked up. Belatedly, St. Clare remembers what I have already recalled. "My Lord, Mr. Manley is dyslexic and is as a result unable to read any part of this statement aloud."

Quigg says, "I'm sorry, My Lord. Of course I would be happy to read it on Mr. Manley's behalf."

And I realize she did know, Quigg, about his dyslexia. This moment has been choreographed to perfection. Tyson Manley looks up at Quigg as she removes the statement in front of him and carries it back to her desk. His entire body is erect, his anger palpable. His eyes are filled with fury, his face with unadulterated hate. This is how he looked at the

Sports Ground as he was killing my son. This was the expression on his face as he stabbed Ryan. This was the face Sweetie looked into after he'd listened to Ryan's innocent message left on her phone, when he returned to her house later with his friends and they did what they did. It may also have been the expression on his face when he finished crying after his brother was shot, maybe the exact expression every teacher who asked him to read aloud in front of the class has seen. Quigg takes her time, slowly turns around to face him.

I feel Lloydie squeezing my hand and I squeeze his. This is the monster we both expected.

Quigg says, "Mr. Manley . . ."

He says, "You think you're so smart, don't you?"

"I'm sorry?"

"No you're not. You're not sorry. You think you can tell me what to do? That they can?" He indicates the jury. "That he can?" He indicates the judge.

St. Clare stands in a panic, says, "My Lord—"

But the judge raises a finger, momentarily silencing him.

"You wanna know why man's here? I'm here 'cause every morning the screws wake me up and a van comes to collect me. I'm here 'cause them guards there march me through the dungeons and bring me to this room. You think I care if you find me guilty? Every day I wake up, that I open my eyes is a blessing; one day more and I give thanks. You know how many of my bredrins, my blood, I seen killed? The number of funerals I been to? The number I couldn't make? Every time I leave my yard, walk street, step offa bus or outta car could be my last moment and I'm ready, I'm ready to die; man, I been ready to die for years. You think I'm gonna start bawling 'cause this court says I'm a bad boy? Go on, do your worst, find me guilty. Give man ten years, fifteen years, gimme a life sentence, 'cause that's exactly what you'll gimme: life. I'll do my bird, and I'll be alive till you set me back out on the street. This system don't mean shit!"

St. Clare says, "My Lord, I really must insist on an adjournment—"

Manley says, "I don't need no adjournment. I ain't answering no more dumb-ass questions."

The judge calls for a break anyway. We gather quietly in the stairwell and wait. Ms. Manley, the young man with her, and De-Niro head down the staircase. Ricardo whispers to Luke, "He's going down. Good!"

I agree he's going down, but I can't decide now whether I think it's a good thing or not.

Nipa asks, "Have you written the second statement yet?" I shake my head. "You probably need to do it tonight. After Manley, there's just the closing statements to go. Tomorrow may be the last day."

"I'll do it tonight," I say.

"What are you going to put in it?" Lorna asks.

"That's why I haven't done it yet," I say. "I don't really know."

When we are called back in, Quigg has no further questions for the defendant, and for the first time, I feel empathy toward St. Clare, who looks like a person feigning optimism. He says he has no further questions for his client. As for Tyson Manley, it's as if having had his explosion, having allowed the jury to really see beneath the facade, he can no longer be bothered to pretend, or maybe he no longer sees the point, so he just stands in the dock looking pissed off.

It is just after four now and Quigg asks for an adjournment till the morning to deliver her closing statement. The judge agrees. Ms. Manley and her son have not returned to the public gallery following the break. As Tyson Manley waits to be led from the stand, his eyes search the gallery for them, is disappointed, I think, not to find them there. For the briefest moment, his eyes meet mine. For me, the connection is electric though nothing in his expression changes. He does not take the opportunity, brief as it is, to smile or nod in acknowledgment, or even better, burst into tears of remorse, just looks at me as he has looked out on the proceedings for the last week or so, with complete indifference. I tug off my wig and stand so he can see me clearly, my sparsely tufted scalp, recent laceration, and all. I want him to see, to know. I see some shift inside him, small but present. I can't assess it clearly, but it is not to do with embarrassment or regret or restoration, it is something else I'm not entirely certain of, but I think is to do with respect. That's what I see in his eyes as he looks at me for a few seconds only, then allows the guards to lead him away.

10

LLOYDIE AND I DECIDE TO travel back on the tube with Lorna to her place. It is the beginning of the rush hour and the three of us stand together inside the carriage, steadying ourselves around a bar. I say, "Sending him to prison isn't a punishment."

Lorna asks, "What would you like them to do?"

"I don't know," I say. "Something that serves some purpose, that either changes him or punishes him in a way that means it's a proper punishment."

"What you heard in that courtroom was bravado," Lorna says. "No seventeen-year-old boy wants to go to prison and stay in there till he's in his thirties. It's a wasted life."

"But it is a life," I say. "That's the point he was making, that he'll be in prison, but he'll be alive."

Lloydie says, "Well, if he was that eager, I'm surprised he never just pleaded guilty in the first place."

We stop at Mothercare when we get off the tube. We are in there for an hour, trying to remember the things a newborn needs, prioritizing at Lorna's insistence that we try not to overwhelm Sweetie. In the end, she buys wipes and nappies, toiletries, and a clothing gift set for baby girls. We buy a warm coat and a couple of blankets, and because Lloydie picked it up from a display at the front counter and kept it in his hands the whole time we were walking around, a cute, pink, impossibly soft bed-buddy.

I had forgotten the feel of Mothercare, the brightness and colors and light, the chatter and laughter of little ones, blooming mums-to-be, so many of them and all in one space. It is a place of newness and beginnings and growth, mothers filled with love and aspirations and hope. It feels like the antithesis of this trial that has monopolized my life, that has in its own way been as traumatic as the event, filled me with loathing, sadness, and despair. While they are bagging up our purchases and we are trying to decide how best to carry the load between us, I realize I am done with it. I will not return tomorrow for the closing statements. I'm happy to not be there when the jury brings in the verdict. I will do something other. I don't want to witness the decimation of another life. I want to build something.

On the walk back I say, "I'm going to start a charity in Ryan's name. I haven't thought it through properly, but I was thinking maybe something to help young people who want to change their lives, find a way back into society, open doors."

Lorna stops walking. She begins to cry. Then hugs me. We stop, wait for her to compose herself, which she does after a time, then laughs, wiping her eyes. "'S about time you did something constructive with yourself."

I smile at her. "I've no idea where to start. I'll have to do some research."

"I can do some of it," Lloydie says. "I've got the time."

"It'll be his legacy," I say.

From the front doorstep outside Lorna's home, I can hear the baby crying. The sound is distinctly newborn, shrill, a tiny tongue oscillating against the roof of a mouth. Lorna puts her bags down in the passage, opens the living room door, heads in. Sweetie is standing in the middle of the room cradling the baby, rocking her too fast, as distressed as the baby she is trying to calm down.

"She just won't stop crying," she says. "I've fed her and I've changed her. I dunno why she won't just stop."

Lorna takes off her coat, throws it onto the chair. "Let me take her," she says. "Where's Kwame?"

"He had to move his car. They were gonna clamp it."

Sweetie hands the baby over. "Hello," Lorna says, holding her under the armpits as she dangles her, gently raising her up and down. Her cries begin to subside immediately.

"She can probably feel your stress," I say to Sweetie without taking my eyes off the baby. "It's harder to calm them down when you're stressed out."

Lorna puts the baby to her shoulder, begins to rub her tiny back.

"She might just have wind," I say, unable to stop looking. I feel Lloydie follow me around, so we are both standing behind Lorna, staring at this baby's face. She looks as upset as only a baby can, utterly distraught, as though she's taken all a person can bear, has no idea how she's expected to go on.

Lloydie says, "My God, she's beautiful."

She is. I wish I wasn't doing it but I am, searching that tiny face, remembering my son, looking for any resemblance.

He was the same shade pretty much as Sweetie, muscovado brown. This baby is several shades lighter, but the tiny dark strip across the tip of her ear indicates that will change. Lorna was right, she looks like a newborn baby. I straighten up. The only feature on her face that bears a relation to any person living or dead appears to be her mouth. She has her mother's mouth. I take off my coat, put it on the chair beside Lorna's. "Can I hold her?" I ask.

Lloydie says to me, "You should wash your hands."

I do. Lloydie is standing in exactly the same spot I left him in when I return. Sweetie is no longer in the room. "Let me have a hold," I say to Lorna.

She is calmer now. Ryan was a calm baby. She is smaller than he was, so light, almost nothing, and it comes, the intensity of feeling that came with holding Ryan. It is like standing in his bedroom drawing the curtain and raising a draft. I smile at Lloydie. He is transfixed. "Do you want to hold her?" I ask. He wants to, I can see in his eyes he longs to, but he's scared, like he was with his son when he was born, scared his huge hands, mammoth in comparison with this minute fragile being, might harm her by accident.

"Not yet," he says. "She needs to grow a bit, get bigger first. Then I will."

She's ours. He's thinking ahead, to the future, sees this beautiful baby in it. Sweetie comes back into the room. She has neatened her hair, freshened up; I smell newly applied deodorant. I watched a documentary about an adoption fair some time ago. It made me feel quite sad, all those poor mites hoping to be adopted, who turned up to the fair trying to be the best they could be, all neat and tidy and nervous smiles, hoping the prospective adoptive parents attending might like them enough to want to keep them. That's what I'm reminded of when I look at Sweetie. She is stripped of the bravado I saw the first time I met her in my kitchen, and without it she is just an awkward, vulnerable teenage girl.

"She looks just like you," I say to her.

Sweetie smiles. She's gorgeous, this girl. That smile must have been what bedazzled my son.

"Just like you," Lloydie says. "Beautiful."

"Thanks."

"Do you have a name for her?" I ask.

She shakes her head. "I've got a couple of names in my head, but I don't think they suit her. I'm still thinking about it."

"I've got a dictionary of baby names at home," I say. "I'll bring it up in the morning."

She smiles again, says, "Cool."

My notebook is leaned against my raised knees in front of me. I need to write that statement tonight, need to find the words. I can hear the sound of Lloydie moving around in the loft above me, shifting boxes and big stuff, bringing things down. He is brushing dust off himself when he finally comes into the bedroom. He smiles at me. He looks like he has purpose.

"I've brought the pieces of Ryan's cot down," he says. "I hope all the screws are still there. I'm gonna start painting it in the morning. Should be dry in a couple of days."

"I knew that was what you were doing."

"Maybe we can go shopping for a mattress tomorrow?"

"Okay."

"What you doing?"

"Nothing. I've done a rough draft of that second Victim

Personal Statement. I just need to do a proper copy. I'll give it to Nipa when she comes in the morning."

"Does she know we're not coming?"

"Yes. I told her. It's fine."

"I'm gonna have my shower. I'll read it when I come out."

I scrub out what I have written, begin again. "Okay."

VICTIM PERSONAL STATEMENT (2ND)

You said your dream was to be alive when you're older. My son is no longer alive, but he would have approved of your dream. He wanted the same thing, not just for himself, but for every living thing, and that would have included you. With Ryan in mind, I hope your dream comes true. I also hope with all my heart that one day you will come to understand what you have done, but I know you can never understand what you have done till you have learned to care. And for that reason, my greatest wish for you is love.

Acknowledgments

EVERYONE WHO HAS SUPPORTED ME during the writing of
The Mother, who has provided the essential space, friendship,
humor, shoulder, ears, and encouragement to enable me to
get to The End, you have my heartfelt thanks and gratitude
always.

I am indebted to my first readers—Danielle Acquah,
Olcay Aniker, Corinne Dowd, Colin Edwards, Elizabeth Gal-
loway, and Jaclyn Griffiths—for their insightful feedback and
suggestions that helped to shape this novel. For invaluable
discussions, pointers, and information, thank you very much
to Shawn Bulbulia-McClean, Daryll Ellick, Paul Etheridge,
Vicky Guedalla, Mark Ashford, Alistair Fruish, and Stephen
Graham. For the germination of time itself, thank you to
Jindra Adamova and Angelo Iuliano. And to Sukti Neogi,
planter of seeds, thank you too.

For generosity of spirit, advice, and practical assistance,
I would very much like to thank Robin Lockhart of Catalyst
in Communities. I am indebted to Mandisa Knights for legal
advice and her endeavors to keep me watertight. I apologize

for liberties I have taken with that advice and embrace any resulting errors as mine alone. I would very much like to thank Hakim Kayizzi from East London for his inestimable assistance. I am also deeply grateful to Yvonne Lawson, of the Godwin Lawson Foundation, for being so receptive and open to the discussions that have had a huge impact on this novel.

Eve White, my agent, thank you for your inexhaustible optimism and your belief in my writing. Tracy Sherrod, Editorial Director at Amistad, thank you for your continued support, enthusiasm, and advice. And Sam Humphreys, Associate Publisher at Mantle, Pan Macmillan, thank you very much for your patience, guidance, and sound judgment. Much appreciated.

About the Author

YVVETTE EDWARDS, the author of the highly praised *A Cupboard Full of Coats*, has lived in London all her life. She resides in the East End and is married with three daughters and a stepson. *The Mother* is her second novel.

ALSO BY YVVETTE EDWARDS

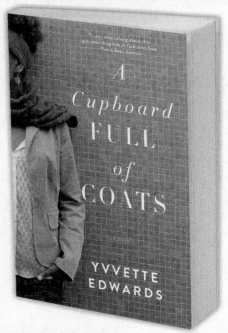

A CUPBOARD FULL OF COATS
A Novel
Available in Paperback and E-book

Longlisted for the Man Booker Prize • Shortlisted for the Commonwealth Prize

"In this potent mystery . . . Edwards makes us greedy for the full story." —*New York Times*

Plagued by guilt, paralyzed by shame, Jinx has spent the years since her mother's death alone, estranged from her husband, withdrawn from her son, and entrenched in a childhood home filled with fierce and violent memories. When Lemon, an old family friend, appears, he seduces Jinx with a heady mix of powerful storytelling and tender care. What follows is a tense and passionate weekend, as the two join forces to unravel the tragedy that binds them.

Expertly woven and perfectly paced, *A Cupboard Full of Coats* is both a heartbreaking family drama and a riveting mystery, with a cast of characters who linger in the mind and the heart long after the last page has been turned.